A Candlelight
Ecstasy Romance®

"DON'T RUN AWAY. IT WON'T DO ANY GOOD."

Miles gently took her hand. "I just told you I love you. Doesn't that mean anything at all?"

Claire tried not to hear the passion in his voice. "Miles, you're only here for two weeks. What happens after that? Do you just pack up and leave me with a broken heart?"

"Of course not. You'd come with me."

"But Charleston is my home! I can't leave my friends and the place I've grown to love—"

"Stop fooling yourself, Claire! We're meant to be together. And deep down inside, you know it."

"I don't know anything of the kind!"

"Then I'll prove it to you. What do you feel when I touch you? What does your heart tell you when we kiss? You belong to me, Claire, and I'm not going to let you go!"

CANDLELIGHT ECSTASY CLASSIC ROMANCES

CANDLELIGHT ECSTASY ROMANCES®

GARDEN OF ENCHANTMENT

Christine King

A CANDLELIGHT ECSTASY ROMANCE®

Published by
Dell Publishing Co., Inc.
1 Dag Hammarskjold Plaza
New York, New York 10017

Dell ® TM 681510, Dell Publishing Co., Inc.

Candlelight Ecstasy Romance®, 1,203,540, is a registered trademark of Dell Publishing Co., Inc., New York, New York.

ISBN: 0-440-12934-6

Printed in the United States of America

January 1987

10 9 8 7 6 5 4 3 2 1

WFH

To Darlene Soltess,
One of life's real heroines

To Our Readers:

We have been delighted with your enthusiastic response to Candlelight Ecstasy Romances®, and we thank you for the interest you have shown in this exciting series.

In the upcoming months we will continue to present the distinctive sensuous love stories you have come to expect only from Ecstasy. We look forward to bringing you many more books from your favorite authors and also the very finest work from new authors of contemporary romantic fiction.

As always, we are striving to present the unique, absorbing love stories that you enjoy most—books that are more than ordinary romance. Your suggestions and comments are always welcome. Please write to us at the address below.

Sincerely,

The Editors
Candlelight Romances
1 Dag Hammarskjold Plaza
New York, New York 10017

GARDEN OF
ENCHANTMENT

CHAPTER ONE

"Claire? *Claire!* Are you listening to me?" asked the tall, willowy blond woman standing impatiently in the doorway.

Claire Ashley skillfully drove a nail into the wall and proceeded to hang the picture. Then she stepped back and eyed the painting critically.

It's perfect, she thought as she studied the watercolor. She had found it hiding in a corner of her attic, and it was made for that wall.

Then a small frown creased her normally smooth brow. She tilted the painting ever so slightly to the left and turned back to Sarah, her friend.

"I'm listening," she said mildly. "But I just don't understand why you're so upset. Nothing like that can happen here."

"You haven't heard a word I've said!" Sarah told her accusingly. A few minutes earlier, she had burst in on Claire with a wild story about a sleek modern hotel being built in the heart of historic Charleston. "If you *had* been listening, you'd know why I'm so upset."

Claire sat down on an antique mahogany chair and looked around the dining room of her Charleston "double house" with pleasure. The restoration of this room had only been finished for a few days, and she still wasn't used to the beauty she had found beneath the layers of muddy paint and dark wallpaper that had been added by successive generations of Ashleys.

Sarah was right, Claire thought ruefully. She hadn't really been listening. Her mind had been filled with thoughts of her next restoration project.

"I'm sorry," she said contritely. She glanced down at her watch, then jumped to her feet. "It's past ten o'clock. I've got to get the beds made. Come upstairs with me and tell me about it again—in detail, this time. I promise I'll listen."

Claire gave Sarah a winsome smile and led the way across the wide hall and up the graceful, curving staircase to the second floor.

Sarah took one look at Claire and her anger melted away. Who could be angry with Claire when she smiled like that? Sarah thought with a sigh. What a pity she didn't smile more often.

But then, Sarah told herself, Claire was completely immersed in the restoration of this house of hers, and that gave her little reason to smile. Restoring a house of this size took a great deal of money—money Claire didn't have. Sarah shook her head and wished, not for the first time, that Claire weren't so independent.

She and Claire had been friends since the first summer Claire came to Charleston to stay with her grandmother. During that summer and each summer thereafter, the two girls had giggled and dreamed and grown up together. Now that Claire lived permanently in Charleston, they were better friends than ever, despite their contrasting personalities.

Sarah was a stunning blonde with a bubbling personality. She was as outgoing as Claire was reserved. Claire was as physically beautiful as Sarah, but it often took a second glance to note the gentleness of Claire's eyes and the tenderness of her lips. Masses of dark brown hair fell in thick, silky waves to her shoulders, framing the classic planes of her face. Her soft gray eyes were the dreamy, vague eyes of a romantic who sees things others don't.

Sarah shook her head as she followed Claire into one of the second-floor bedrooms. Time and time again, she had offered to arrange dates for Claire. Dinner dates, movie dates, picnics—anything to get Claire involved with men.

And time and time again, Claire had refused. Though her face, smooth and young looking, didn't show the heartaches she had suffered as a child, she had suffered them nonetheless. Now that she was older and had some control over her life, she intended to suffer no more. Emotional entanglements, she had decided long ago, were not for her. Perhaps that was why, at twenty-five, she looked years younger. She had deliberately kept herself aloof from the kind of life most women her age lived.

I've got to get her to go out more, Sarah thought to herself. The Fancy Dress Ball at the Ashley Plantation is coming up. She should be going—it's being given by her cousin—but with Claire, you never know.

I'll make sure she attends, Sarah vowed, and somehow I'll make sure she has a good time.

"Sit down," Claire suggested, gesturing vaguely toward a chair.

Sarah perched on a small love seat in front of tall, lovely windows that overlooked a walled-in garden. She watched for a moment as Claire stripped the sheets from the bed.

13

"You can't really enjoy this," she burst out suddenly.

"Enjoy what?" Claire asked. She put the dirty sheets into a laundry basket, then picked up the clean sheets and flipped one open.

"Cleaning up after people you don't know," Sarah told her. "You can't enjoy making beds for them and picking up their dirty towels and serving them breakfast every morning."

Claire smoothed the sheets into place. "I don't mind it," she said. "Running a bed and breakfast gives me a chance to work on this house, and that's what's important to me right now."

"But you have strangers trooping in and out of here all the time!" Sarah said a little helplessly. "I don't know how you can stand it."

"I've met some very nice people," Claire replied. She and Sarah had had this conversation before. "People who are thrilled to be staying in a house like this, even if it's only for a night or two." She finished making the bed and began straightening up the room.

"Your grandmother would turn over in her grave if she knew what you were doing," Sarah grumbled.

Claire stopped what she was doing and turned to look at Sarah. "My grandmother was a very practical woman," she told her friend. "She wouldn't mind at all if she thought this was the best way to keep the house in the family."

"Well, the least you can do is hire a maid to help you," Sarah told her crossly. "Then you wouldn't have to do everything yourself."

"I could do that, but maids cost money," Claire pointed out, "and I'd much rather spend money on the house."

"I know that, but—"

Claire held up her hand to stop Sarah from saying anything else. "Now, what did you want to tell me about?" she asked.

Sarah sighed and gave up. She knew arguing with Claire wouldn't do any good. It never had, and it probably never would.

"I went over to Gibbes and Boone before the office opened this morning," she said—it was the law firm in which her brother was a partner—"to see if Michael had finished drawing up the contract for the house on Legare Street I was telling you about." She made a face. "Naturally, he wouldn't say anything. Sometimes I think he takes this lawyer-client-confidentiality stuff too seriously. I'm his sister, after all," she said a little indignantly. "Fortunately, I managed to get it out of one of the secretaries."

"Get what out of one of the secretaries?" Claire asked patiently. She was used to Sarah's way of telling things.

"I peeked in one of the conference rooms," Sarah went on, completely ignoring Claire's question, "and there sat this perfectly dreadful man. He was reading some long document and looked absolutely furious." She shuddered dramatically. "I wouldn't want to meet him in a dark alley. Of course I had to find out who he was," she said with a sideward glance at Claire.

"Of course," Claire put in dryly.

Sarah liked men and attracted them in a way that most women would envy. But not Claire. She marveled at the parade of good-looking men through Sarah's life, but she wasn't the least bit jealous. Swift hellos and good-byes weren't for her. She'd known too many of them already.

"I asked Michael who he was," Sarah told Claire, "but

15

he wouldn't tell me. In fact, he seemed a little put out by my question. He said—you know how stuffy Michael can be—he said, 'Sarah, I've told you time and time again, I cannot discuss anything that takes place in this office.' "

Claire laughed a little as Sarah imitated her straitlaced brother.

"So I went to one of the secretaries, and she told me all about that awful-looking man—in confidence, of course. Michael would probably fire her if he knew."

"Then you shouldn't be telling me any of this," Claire interrupted firmly.

"Oh yes, I should. For one thing, it concerns you, and for another, I need your help. This man works for a company that puts up those modern glass and steel hotels. And," Sarah finished with dismal triumph, "he wants to put one up in the heart of Charleston."

"I'm sure Michael told him that was impossible," Claire said calmly. "Charleston has very strict zoning laws."

"I know that," Sarah said a little impatiently. "But this man's company has a flock of high-powered lawyers who have apparently found a loophole in the law."

"A loophole?" Claire echoed in astonishment. "That's impossible. There couldn't be."

"Well, there is. The secretary couldn't explain it to me, but it's enough to let this man put up his miserable hotel. It will ruin Charleston," she wailed.

Claire shook her head. "We'll have the zoning law revised and the loophole closed," she said practically. "That's all there is to it."

"Maybe," Sarah said glumly. "If we have the time. I don't know how long something like that would take."

"You're a member of the Preservation Society," Claire

pointed out. "You should be telling *them* about this, not me."

"Oh, I will. You needn't worry about that. But you see"—she hesitated for a moment—"one of the houses he wants to buy is yours."

"Mine!" Claire began to laugh. "Well then, there's no problem. I'd never sell this house to anyone. It's the only real home I've ever had, and I'm going to keep it."

Claire's father had left Charleston for college and had never come back. After graduation, he had married and joined the army, but that meant his family had moved frequently. Claire had hated the constant moving and at age nineteen, after two years of college herself, she had returned to Charleston to live with her grandmother and put down her roots in earnest. She was hoping to find the security that had eluded her all her life. Three years later, her grandmother had died, leaving Claire her eighteenth-century house and what little money she possessed.

For Claire, it was as if the house had been given to her as a trust. Ashleys had always lived in this house, and she had no intention of breaking the line. Lovingly, she began to repair and restore the house, not minding that it took all her money and most of her time. Nothing could induce her to part with it.

"I'll never sell," Claire repeated emphatically, "and neither will anyone else when they find out why this man wants to buy."

"I wish I were as sure of that as you are," Sarah said unhappily. "He's already approached the Bowens next door, and apparently they're considering his offer. They're elderly, they can't afford to keep up the house, and they have no children or grandchildren to leave it to anyway. I'm sure his offer is very tempting."

"I'll talk to them," Claire promised, "but I don't think there's any reason to worry. One house won't do him any good. He'd have to buy several before there'd be enough room for a hotel. These lots are very narrow."

That was a fact of history and one of the reasons for Charleston's charm. The tall, slender houses with their tiered piazzas were built sideways to save space for their walled gardens.

"Money talks," Sarah said unhappily. "He's the kind of man who gets what he wants. If you'd seen him, you'd know what I mean. He'll just keep offering more and more money until people can't afford *not* to sell to him."

Claire shook her head. "The company he works for will never go along with that. He'll have to give up if his plans become economically unfeasible," she said shrewdly. "What's his name?"

"I don't remember. The secretary told me, but I was so unnerved I didn't catch it. It's probably some typical Yankee name," Sarah said spitefully. "He was no southern gentleman, that's for sure."

Claire smiled to herself. Sarah and her family were dyed-in-the-wool southerners, and she sometimes got the idea they hadn't yet gotten over the Civil War.

"I'm surprised Michael is having anything to do with this person," Claire said. "After all, he's a member of the Preservation Society, too."

Sarah brightened. "He's not having anything to do with him. That's the one bit of good news the secretary told me. Apparently, Michael told this man that Gibbes and Boone absolutely would not represent his company. That's probably why he looked so annoyed when I saw him."

"If he has his own lawyers, why does he want Michael?"

"Well," Sarah speculated, "it would be quite a feather in his cap to be represented by Charleston's leading law firm. Besides," she went on a little vaguely, "there's a law about local counsel. While he's in South Carolina, he's got to be represented by someone who is a member of the South Carolina bar."

"Well," Claire said, "I don't think there's anything to worry about, but I'll talk to the Bowens today or tomorrow."

"Do it soon!" Sarah implored. "Before they have a chance to sign anything. If he even gets a foot in the door, who knows what will happen!"

"And you get hold of the people you know who can take action against this man," Claire put in. "I'm sure we can stop him. Now, try not to worry."

"I wish I had your confidence," Sarah told her grimly. "If you'd seen him, you'd know why I'm worried. He looked so determined."

"So are we," Claire pointed out. "And thanks to you, we're forewarned. You know the old saying—"

" 'Forewarned is forearmed,' " Sarah quoted, with a return of some of her natural gaiety. She got up to leave. "I'll call you when I know something."

Claire listened for a moment as Sarah hurried down the stairs. The front door tinkled musically as she let herself out. The sound of the bell, which Claire had installed to announce the arrival of her guests, reminded her that she had work to do. She still had the bathrooms to clean, she wanted to check the Blue Room, too, to make sure it was ready for the guest who was arriving that afternoon.

Her eyes brightened as she looked around the exquisitely furnished room. It was the finest of her four bedrooms, and it was also the most expensive. There was a priceless Aubusson rug on the floor and antique Fortuny silk curtains hung at the windows; and the furniture was Ashley family heirlooms.

Claire priced the bedroom accordingly high, and so, even though it was the only one of her bedrooms with a private bath, she had few requests for it. Today, however, a guest who hadn't blanched at the room rate was arriving, and he had reserved the room for two whole weeks!

Claire smiled a little ruefully to herself as she added up the dollars in her head. As Sarah said, she always needed money.

By two thirty, Claire had finished all her chores. The house was spotless, a coconut pound cake had been made, and fresh flowers were scenting the air in the Blue Room.

As a reward, she sat down at the mahogany Sheraton desk that graced her wide hallway and began working on the plans for the third floor of her house. She became so lost in her work that, twenty minutes later, she didn't hear the doorbell when it rang again.

A tall, well-dressed man stepped over the threshold, but he stopped as soon as he caught sight of Claire bent industriously over her desk. With his hand still on the doorknob and the door still open, he stared at her. He couldn't seem to tear his eyes away. A shaft of sunlight streaming in from a nearby window shone down on her, highlighting her rich, thick hair and the creamy, camellia-white color of her skin. With irrational certainty, he knew he was about to meet someone very special.

His eyes roamed wonderingly over her face, noting its

20

delicate oval shape and her well-shaped, sensuous mouth. Though her eyes were hidden from him by dark, curling lashes, he was sure they would be warm and expressive. Her hair, which he suddenly wanted to caress, tumbled gracefully in silky waves to her shoulders.

As he watched her, she plucked a full-blown rose from the vase in front of her. With gentleness that communicated itself to him, she brought the fragile flower to her nose and sniffed its sweetness. Then she brushed the flower against her cheek so that she could feel its softness next to her skin.

She's beautiful, he thought. Everything about her is beautiful.

He felt a little stunned by his reaction to her. Never before had he felt the sudden attraction he was feeling now. Crazy though it seemed, he wanted to cross the room, sweep her up into his arms, and carry her off to a place where the two of them could be completely alone.

All at once, Claire sensed his presence. She looked up, saw him standing in the doorway, and jumped.

With the sun shining in her eyes, she couldn't see his face clearly, but something in the way he was standing warned her of danger. When he didn't move, she felt a sudden surge of panic.

This man means trouble, she thought. For a second she wanted to run.

Then he seemed to remember where he was. Slowly and a little ominously, it seemed to her, he closed the door behind him. To Claire, the closing of the door had a very final sound to it. She wasn't quite sure why, but she found his presence very disturbing. She supposed it had to do with the aura of power and confidence he gave off,

21

an aura she could feel even though she hadn't yet clearly seen his face.

He took a step forward and their eyes met.

"Good morning," she said a little breathlessly.

They stared at each other for a very long moment. Claire wanted to look away, but she couldn't. There was something magnetic about him that kept her from breaking through the tension that was building between them.

Again, panic swept over her. She stood up, instinctively poised for flight. Unnoticed by either of them, her pencil rolled off the desk and fell to the floor.

Then he took another step forward, a step that brought him into the sunlight, and her illusion of danger burst.

Standing in front of her, giving her a warm smile, was a very attractive man. There was nothing the least bit frightening about him.

He moved toward her, and as he got closer he noticed that pale rose-pink had suffused her cheeks and her warm gray eyes, which were still regarding him warily.

She's a proper southern lady, he thought. Cool and reserved on the outside—but underneath? Underneath, he was sure there beat the heart of a desirable and desiring woman.

It was Claire who finally broke the silence.

"May I help you?" she asked. As she uttered the words, her voice sounded chilly, even to her. She didn't want to be unfriendly, but she didn't want him to realize just how attractive and how alarming she found him, either.

He gave her a smile that seemed to light up the room. At the sight of it, Claire frowned slightly and mentally shook herself. How silly could she be? A smile was a smile. There was no reason why she should suddenly feel warm all over.

"I'm Miles Sinclair," he said easily. "I have a reservation for one of your rooms."

"Oh yes, Mr. Sinclair," Claire began, trying to sound as composed as he did.

"Call me Miles," he interrupted, "and you are—"

"Claire," she supplied. She was surprised at herself. Normally she liked to maintain a more formal relationship with her guests. "I'm Claire Ashley."

"You're Claire Ashley," he repeated slowly. His warm, dark eyes swept her face. "I had no idea you'd be so young . . . or so beautiful."

Claire felt herself blush at his intimate words. And his eyes—she quickly stopped herself from thinking about the look in his eyes.

"Would you like to see your room?" she asked to put them on a more professional level.

With an effort, he wrenched his eyes from her face and looked around him. "If it's as lovely as this hall, I'm sure I'll like it. Lead the way."

As he followed her up the curving staircase, Claire was uncomfortably aware of him behind her. She could feel his gaze on her shoulders and back, and she suddenly found herself wishing she was wearing something other than her very ordinary shirtwaist dress.

"Here we are," she said as they entered the Blue Room.

Miles stopped just inside the doorway and looked around him appreciatively.

"I'm overwhelmed," he said as he stared at the huge rice bed at one end of the room. His eyes moved on.

23

"Isn't that a Thomas Elfe chest?" he asked, naming a well-known eighteenth-century Charleston cabinetmaker.

Claire nodded a little proudly. "Do you know much about antiques?"

"Enough to know that it shouldn't be left in a room rented to strangers," he replied.

He began to tour the room, and when he stopped in front of a Chippendale chair, Claire had a chance to study him.

He was a big man, she noted as she took in the lines of his body. He was so big that he seemed almost larger than life. Beneath his impeccably cut gray suit she could almost see the rippling muscles of his shoulders. The suit coat fit perfectly across his back and shoulders and tapered slightly, allowing her to note his trim waist and hips. He obviously patronized a very good tailor.

His hair had once been very dark. Now the black was heavily laced with silver threads. His eyes, set beneath heavy slashes of brow, were a dark, almost liquid brown. The sun had tanned his face, giving him a dashing air.

He had something more than sheer romantic good looks, Claire thought as she studied him. He had that mysterious, indefinable something that made people's heads turn. He had an air of authority, and there was power and confidence in every move he made.

Once he finished his tour of the room, he turned and scrutinized her, just as she had been scrutinizing him.

His eyes lightly touched her hair and face, then traveled slowly downward, noting her pale green cotton dress with its long sleeves and demurely fastened white piqué collar.

Claire flushed—with annoyance, she told herself,

though she was also embarrassed at the way he took in the curves that her simple dress could not conceal.

The pink in her cheeks deepened as his eyes returned to her face, and she read approval in them. She had never before been subjected to such an open appraisal, and she didn't think she liked it. The men of Charleston had more respect for women than to treat them like that, she thought indignantly as she turned away and walked back toward the door.

When she reached the door, she was upset to discover that she was trembling slightly. She turned and gave him an icy look. He was a paying guest, but that didn't give him the right to be too familiar. She was trying to think of a way to put him in his place when he spoke.

"I'm very impressed," he told her. He walked over to the bed and perched on the edge of it. "This is a beautiful room."

At his words, some of the chilliness left Claire's eyes. She heard nothing but sincerity in his voice. Anyone who appreciated the beauty of one of Charleston's historic houses couldn't be all bad, she rationalized to herself. But she had no intention of forgiving him for the bad-mannered way he had looked her up and down, even though she was a little more inclined to overlook it.

"I'm glad you like it," she said.

"How many bedrooms do you rent out?" he asked, sounding as if he really wanted to know.

"Only four," she told him, "though I'm hoping to have six by this time next year. I'm in the process of getting two more ready on the third floor, but restoring a house room by room takes a lot of time."

Miles nodded sympathetically. "And a great deal of money," he added.

"Exactly," Claire told him with a smile.

"In some cases, I'd wonder if it's worth all the trouble and expense," he said.

"Of course it's worth it!" she said indignantly, her smile fading. "This house was built before the Revolution. It's of great interest historically and architecturally." Her words tumbled over themselves. "It would be a crime to let it deteriorate any further."

"I seem to have struck a nerve," Miles said lightly. "I'm sorry, I didn't realize you were such an ardent preservationist. What a waste," he added almost to himself.

"A waste?" Claire echoed coldly. "What do you mean?"

"I mean it's a shame to waste all that enthusiasm"—his voice lowered meaningfully—"and all that passion on a house."

Claire started to speak, but he held up his hand.

"I know, I know," he said. Laughter suddenly twinkled in his eyes. "This isn't just a house. It's an historic and architectural monument."

Claire frowned. "It's also my home," she told him quietly, "and it's very important to me." She sensed that he was laughing at her, and she didn't like it. Just who was he, she asked herself, to come into *her* home and make *her* feel uncomfortable?

"Of course it is," he said more gently. The laughter left his face. "I shouldn't tease you like that—"

"Would you like to see the rest of the house?" she asked quickly. All at once, she wanted to get out of the bedroom.

"Very much," he replied promptly.

"We'll skip the bedrooms and go back downstairs," Claire told him.

"Do you have any other guests now?" he wanted to know as they walked downstairs.

She nodded. "As a matter of fact, I'm full at the moment. I've got two retired schoolteachers here for the spring house-and-garden tours, and a young couple here for a brief vacation. Do you know much about Charleston's double houses?" she asked as she led him into the dining room.

"Not as much as I'd like," he replied truthfully.

Claire nodded and recited the facts and information she normally gave first-time visitors to her house. Usually her tour was a fairly brief one, but Miles was so interested and asked so many questions that she was shocked when she heard the grandfather clock strike four o'clock. They were standing in the hall, and she was telling him about the elaborate staircase.

"I had no idea it was so late!" she exclaimed as the melodious notes died away. The dismay in her voice was obvious.

"Is four o'clock the bewitching hour?" Miles asked. There was an indulgent smile on his face that made her feel very young and very foolish.

"No," she said stiffly, "but I serve tea every afternoon at four. It's such a beautiful day today that I said we'd have it in the garden. So, if you'll excuse me—"

"I won't excuse you," he said promptly. He leaned against the banister and gazed down at her with a look she couldn't identify. "I'm a guest, too, and I don't care anything at all about having tea. Why should I be deprived of your company for the sake of some people I don't know?"

Claire stared at him. She was totally dumbfounded and had no idea what to say.

"But . . ." she began helplessly.

"I tell you what," he said. "If you'll have dinner with me this evening, I'll help you carry things out to the garden. That way everyone will be happy."

"I don't know," Claire said even more helplessly. She wasn't sure she wanted to have dinner with him. The look on his face was making her uncomfortable. He was pushing her, and she didn't like it. "I make it a rule not to socialize with my guests," she added stiffly.

"That's very wise of you," he told her. "But I'm not just any guest. And I'd like to spend some time alone with you."

Claire gave him an even glance. She didn't understand why he was so insistent about having dinner with her. She took a deep breath. "Why?" she asked point-blank.

Miles cupped her chin with his hand and raised it so that she had to look into his eyes. "I think you know the answer to that as well as I do," he said softly.

She pulled away and took a step or two backward. His sheer masculinity was making her feel a little giddy. She opened her mouth to speak, but the tinkling of the front doorbell interrupted whatever she had been about to say. With a feeling of relief, she looked around and saw her two schoolteachers heading toward the staircase.

"My dear," said one of them, "we've had the most wonderful day, but we're absolutely famished! We can't wait to have that tea you promised us." They gave Miles a curious look.

"It will be ready in fifteen minutes," Claire told them. "Just go on out to the garden when you're ready."

As they climbed the stairs to their rooms, she turned

and was about to leave Miles in the hallway. What else could she do? She had her other guests to think of.

He, however, had no intention of being left behind. With a lazy gesture, he reached out and stopped her. As his hand closed over her arm, she felt a tingle slide down her spine.

"What about dinner?" he asked with a smile. It was obvious that he wasn't going to take no for an answer.

To her dismay, Claire felt her heart turn over at the sight of that smile. She didn't want to find herself attracted to any man, let alone Miles Sinclair. He was brash, he was arrogant, and he was a little bit too charming for her peace of mind. After years of struggling, she was happy with her life, and she didn't want anything— particularly a man—to complicate it.

"Well?" he asked insistently.

"All right," she said reluctantly. It seemed to be the only way she was going to get her work done. "I'll have dinner with you."

He squeezed her arm gently. "Good. Now let's go get that tea ready."

In the kitchen, he stacked cups and saucers and plates onto a tray while she sliced the coconut cake and made the tea. When she was ready, he carried the large tray out to the garden and deposited it on the small table on the terrace. Though he claimed he wasn't interested in tea, he drank two cups and spent the next forty-five minutes talking to the retired teachers. Claire could tell that they were flattered by the interest he was showing them.

Why wouldn't they be? she asked herself. He was an unusually attractive man, and any woman would be affected by his charm. She herself wasn't proving to be immune, she thought with chagrin.

When the two older women left to rest before dinner, Miles poured her another cup of tea, then leaned back in his chair.

"This is a very nice touch," he said appreciatively. "I'm sure your guests love this extra little bit of attention."

"I enjoy it myself," she confessed. She was very aware of the way he was watching her with a steady, unblinking gaze, and she found it disconcerting. She wished he'd look somewhere, anywhere, else. "I like getting to know the people who stay with me."

"I can tell," he said. His eyes were still fixed on her face, and she was definitely beginning to feel uncomfortable. "Southern hospitality is legendary, of course, but you seem to have perfected it. I suppose that's what makes your Ashley House so successful."

"Where did you hear about my bed and breakfast?" she asked curiously. He didn't look like the usual kind of person to stay in a place like hers. He looked more like a man who was used to large suites in five-star hotels.

"Someone I work with stayed here last fall and came back to the office raving about the Ashley House."

"Oh? Who was it?"

Something flickered in his eyes. "His name is Dick York. Does that ring a bell?" He looked at her intently.

Claire shook her head. "No, but your name sounds very familiar to me. When I got your letter, I was sure I'd heard it somewhere, and now that you're here, I'm even more sure of it."

Miles stretched his legs out in front of him and crossed one ankle over the other. "I don't know where you would have heard it," he told her nonchalantly.

"Neither do I," she said, "but it's not a common name. I doubt if there are two of you."

He grinned at that. It was a grin full of the devil, and it was almost irresistible. "I doubt it, too."

"What do you do for a living?" she wanted to know. "Perhaps I read about you in a magazine or a newspaper article."

He uncrossed his legs and shook his head. Something in his manner told her that the question made him uncomfortable. "I don't think that's very likely," he said a little curtly.

Claire looked at him thoughtfully. "What do you do for a living?" she asked again. Her voice was a little more insistent. Perhaps it was time she found out something about this man who was having such a strange effect on her.

At her question, she could have sworn he paused, but it was such an imperceptible pause that, a moment later, she wasn't sure it had happened at all. She *was* sure that something had flickered in his eyes, however.

Why? she wondered. Unconsciously, she sat forward, awaiting his answer. When it came, it was very disappointing.

"I'm in construction."

"Construction?" she echoed blankly as she leaned back in her chair. After the way he had avoided her question, she had been expecting something far more lurid. "You mean you build houses?"

"Something like that," he told her.

"Where are you from?"

"Chicago." This time the answer came more promptly.

"The Windy City. What brought you to Charleston?"

31

He gave her an amused look. He seemed to know why she was asking all these questions.

"I was in Atlanta on business, and when I finished up early, I decided to pay a visit to Charleston. And I must say, I'm glad I did." His eyes, warm on her face, told her exactly why he was glad.

"Charleston's a charming town," she replied demurely. "I'm sure you'll enjoy your stay here."

"I'm sure I will. In fact, I'm enjoying it already. Now, if you're finished playing Twenty Questions, why don't you tell me a little about yourself?"

She began piling dishes on the tray. "There isn't anything to tell."

"I doubt that. A woman like you must have a great deal to say about herself."

"A woman like me?" Claire repeated with some amusement. "What do you mean by that?"

He captured her small hand and held it between his two large ones. At his touch, Claire immediately felt the same tingly sensation that she had experienced earlier. She sat very still, scarcely breathing.

"You're hardly what I'd call an ordinary woman," he told her. His dark eyes caught hers and held them as captive as her hand. "You're beautiful, you're intelligent, you're warm and sensitive. I refuse to believe there's nothing to tell."

"What would you like to know?" she asked softly.

"Well, for starters, why are you so passionately devoted to this house?"

"It's my home," Claire answered. She pulled away and started to put the rest of the dishes on the tray. To her dismay, the cups and saucers rattled a little as she lifted them.

"I know it's your home," he told her, "but you make it sound as if it's the only home you've ever had."

"I suppose that's because it *is* the only home I've ever had," she said evenly. "The only real home, anyway. My father is in the army. We were always on the move when I was growing up. He actually volunteered for assignments! If we were lucky, we stayed in one place for as long as a year. Mostly, though, we weren't lucky, and we moved more often than that."

"That doesn't sound like much of a life for a kid," Miles said sympathetically. Claire stole a look at his face and was surprised by the understanding she saw there.

"Not for this one, anyway." Her voice was light, though she was touched by his obvious sympathy. "My two brothers never seemed to mind, and I got used to it."

Actually, Claire had hated moving from house to house, town to town. The constant uprooting was made worse by the fact that she had no mother—only a series of housekeepers. As soon as she made friends with children her own age or the woman looking after her, she had to leave them. She wasn't very old before she realized it was easier not to have friends at all, at least not good friends. That made saying good-bye much easier.

Miles gave her an understanding look. "I see," he said quietly.

Claire wasn't sure she wanted Miles's sympathy. She stood up. Miles was immediately beside her.

"Don't run away," he said. "I want to know more about you."

She gave him a chilly glance. "I'm taking the dishes into the kitchen. I'd hardly call that running away."

"Wouldn't you?" he asked. "It doesn't matter. You can tell me more about yourself tonight at dinner."

Claire stiffened. "About dinner—" she began.

"Oh, no," he interrupted. He put his hands on her arms. "I have no intention of letting you back out now. We have too much to talk about."

"As far as I'm concerned, we don't have anything to talk about," she said. She tried to give him a dismissive look, a look that would put him in his place, but when their eyes met, she felt something warm and silken flow between them. She stared at him, feeling a strong sense of familiarity—which puzzled her. She didn't know this man. Why did she feel she should?

Miles seemed to read her thoughts with an uncanny ability. "I feel it, too," he told her softly.

Confusion filled her eyes. "What do you feel?" she asked uncertainly.

He didn't answer. Instead, he moved closer, and she knew that he wanted to kiss her. As he leaned toward her, she realized that she *wanted* him to kiss her.

Then, when his lips were only a few tantalizing inches from hers, she came to her senses. A sense of self-preservation that she didn't even know she possessed swept over her, and she stepped backward.

Miles took one look at her face and swore softly to himself. The last thing he wanted to do was frighten her —not when there was so much at stake.

"I have some phone calls to make," he told her, "and I still haven't taken my luggage in. Can you be ready to go to dinner at about seven thirty?"

"Yes," she said, "but—" She was feeling very confused.

"No buts," he told her gently. "I really do have something I want to discuss with you."

."All right," she said. After all, she rationalized to herself, what could happen at dinner?

"Good." He brushed his thumb across her mouth in a gesture that was surprisingly gentle for all its sensuality. As she felt it, Claire's heart began to pound, and a strange heat rushed to her cheeks. "I'll meet you in the hall at seven thirty," he said.

Without another word, he turned and was gone. Claire was left staring at his retreating back.

She pursed her lips a little resentfully. Whether she liked it or not, he seemed determined to become involved in her life—even if he had to steamroll her to do it.

Her instincts had been right, she told herself. He *was* dangerous.

CHAPTER TWO

It wasn't until almost six that evening that Claire suddenly remembered her conversation with Sarah. Meeting Miles had completely swept it from her mind. She called the Bowens to ask if she could stop by and see them for a few moments. Though she let the phone ring several times, there was no answer. Finally, she shrugged and hung up.

There wasn't really any reason to worry, she reassured herself. It wouldn't take the man Sarah had seen in her brother's office long to realize that historic Charleston was not the place for his hotel, and he'd pack up and leave. The Bowens could wait until tomorrow. Right now she had more important things to do. She had to get ready for her dinner date.

Claire didn't go out often, and she was determined to savor bathing and dressing for her date as much as the date itself. She felt like a teen-ager again as she slid into a tub full of bubbly bath water.

Something about Miles Sinclair was making her feel lighthearted and a little nervous. He intrigued her, and all at once, Claire was in the mood to be intrigued. Out of fear of the consequences, she had never before let romance into her life. Why risk heartache when you didn't have to? But now, for one night and one night only, she told herself sternly, a little romance might be fun. A single dinner date couldn't lead to heartbreak. Tonight she would be like Sarah, casually taking what life had to offer.

With a kind of carefree abandon, she hopped out of the bathtub and lavishly smoothed on some body cream, then moved to her dressing table. Slowly she brushed eye shadow onto her eyelids and mascara onto her lashes. She highlighted her cheeks with blush, then painstakingly outlined her lips and filled them in with lipstick. Carefully, so she wouldn't smudge her makeup, she slipped on the dress she had chosen to wear. It was made of silvery-gray silk, a color that brought a sparkle to her eyes.

The dress itself, with its snug bodice and straight skirt, showed off the gentle curves of her body. It had a silver belt that emphasized her slender waist and a low-cut portrait neckline that made her neck seem longer.

She brushed her dark hair till it shone, then added a small antique diamond pendant that had belonged to her grandmother. It sparkled brightly at the base of her throat.

That done, she surveyed herself with approval. Her dress managed to be both tailored and feminine and gave Claire a feeling of sophistication. It also gave her an extra measure of poise, something she felt she needed around Miles. He had fluttered her senses more than once during the afternoon, and instinct told her she would be wise to be on her guard around him.

When Claire walked down the stairs at seven thirty, she found Miles already waiting for her in the hall. He had changed into a dark blue suit that made him look even more imposing than before.

"Good evening," she said a little shyly. There was something about him that was alarmingly, almost frighteningly masculine.

"It's a very good evening," he replied as his eyes slid down her body. At the approval in them, Claire felt a sudden surge of happiness.

He held out his hand to help her down the last few stairs, and without thinking, Claire put her own hand in his. Not for the first time that day, his touch made her tingle. But it reminded her that she found Miles just a little bit too attractive for her own safety. As soon as she reached the hallway, she withdrew her hand and took a step away from him. A man like Miles, urbane, sophisticated, and in town for only a few short weeks was not a candidate for any kind of relationship, in her book. Not if she wanted to avoid the heartache of saying good-bye.

"I've made reservations at a restaurant about three blocks from here," he told her. His eyes were warm on her face. "I hope you don't mind if we walk."

"I'd like that," Claire said a little breathlessly. "I like walking." That way, at least she wouldn't have to see the way he was looking at her.

"Good," he said. "It seems to me that Charleston was made for walking. In the evening, when the traffic has disappeared, it's like stepping back in time."

"Don't tell me you're a romantic," Claire said as he held the door open for her. Her voice was teasing.

"I wouldn't have said so before today," he told her enigmatically. "Before today I would have said I was a hard-nosed businessman without much room for sentiment. But now I'm not so sure."

"Why? What happened today to make you change your mind?" she asked lightly, with a glance up at him.

Miles looked down at her, and at the intensity of his gaze, the lightness disappeared from Claire's face. He raised his hand and gently touched her hair. Though his touch was as delicate as a butterfly's kiss, it riveted Claire. She stared back at him a little helplessly.

Then they continued through the gathering dusk. Claire forced herself to relax. She tried not to think about what she'd seen in his dark eyes. Instead, she took a deep breath and let the voluptuousness of the Charleston evening seep into her senses.

Don't take him seriously, she warned herself. He's flirting, nothing more. I'd be much better off concentrating on the touch of the breeze off the ocean and the scent of the flowers. They filled the air with a perfume so rich and sweet, it was almost intoxicating.

At the restaurant, Claire nodded to several people she knew. As they smiled and waved back, she couldn't help noticing the curious looks she was getting, especially from the women in the room. Miles was devastatingly attractive, and she was sure everyone was wondering who he was. Her phone would be ringing tomorrow, she thought with some amusement. In a town the size of Charleston, a man like Miles was news.

It wasn't until she slid into her chair that she noticed Sarah and Michael sitting in one of the banquettes not far away. Claire smiled to herself as she noted the expression on her friend's face. Sarah looked more than surprised—she looked shocked. She stared at Claire and Miles as if she couldn't believe her eyes.

Claire couldn't help feeling a little smug. Sarah was always trying to fix her up with men she didn't want to meet, and now here she was on a date with one of the most gorgeous men either of them had ever seen.

39

"Who's that?" Miles asked when Sarah halfheartedly waved back.

"A friend of mine," Claire replied as they reached their table. "I think I'll go over and say hello to her."

Miles put a hand on her arm. At his touch, Claire felt herself turn very still.

"Don't," he commanded her. "You can talk to her tomorrow." He held the chair, and Claire slid into it. "I had to share you with those schoolteachers this afternoon, and I'm not going to share you tonight." He sat down across from her, moving her own chair so that his broad shoulders blocked her view of Sarah.

Claire knew she ought to resent his words. Normally, she hated being told what to do. But something in his eyes, something warm and persuasive, kept her from saying a word. A little confused by her sudden lack of independence, she picked up the menu. As she stared blankly at the items it listed, she tried to get her feelings in order.

"Would you like a drink?" Miles asked.

"Some sherry, please," she answered, still staring at the menu.

"To Charleston," he said when their cocktails arrived. He raised his glass. "And you," he added softly.

The look on his face brought a faint flush of pink to her face. She looked away quickly and focused on a spot just behind his right shoulder. She hurriedly took a sip of her drink, then returned to the menu. Miles watched her with a faint smile on his face.

"Put that damned thing down," he ordered her a few moments later. With a sure, deft movement, he took the menu from her hands and placed it beside his plate. "You can't hide behind it all evening."

"I wasn't hiding behind it," Claire protested immediately, though that was exactly what she had been doing. The fact that Miles realized it made her feel a little foolish. "I was just—"

"Of course you were hiding behind it," he interrupted impatiently. "And in a way, I don't blame you." He caught her eyes with his and held them until the silence seemed to stretch tightly between them.

Claire finally dragged her eyes from his. "What do you mean?" she asked breathlessly.

"Things are happening very quickly," he replied. His eyes were still fixed on her face.

Claire looked at him. "Nothing is happening," she said at once. She knew she spoke too firmly and a little too loudly, but she couldn't help it. His words had thrown her off balance.

He reached across the table and took her hand. "Then why did you agree to have dinner with me?" he asked as he caressed her fingers with his own.

"Because," she stammered as her hand began to tingle, "because you said you had something you wanted to discuss with me." She didn't like the way he was looking at her. His eyes were so warm, they were unnerving.

"Is that the reason?" he wanted to know. His voice was low and almost intimate in tone. "Or did you come because you're attracted to me? I know I'm attracted to you." His voice dropped even lower. "I'm very attracted to you."

Claire stared at him for a long moment. All kinds of emotions, from panic to elation, were flitting through her mind. Even though she didn't want to get involved with someone like Miles, even though she didn't want to risk being hurt, she couldn't help being a little flattered by his interest in her.

"I don't know what you're talking about," she said finally. She tried to make her voice icy, but a certain breathlessness robbed the words of most of their tartness.

His eyes swept her face. "You must know," he said gently. "It won't do either of us any good to ignore what we're feeling." His voice grew stronger. "Besides, I won't let you hide from it. Now that I've found you, I don't want to let you go."

Claire gazed at him helplessly. He looked so determined, so positive. She had never met a man before with this much self-confidence. It was almost alarming.

"I'm not yours to let go or not let go," she said finally. Her voice was defiant.

"Not yet," he agreed with annoying calmness. "But you will be, and soon."

His words made her angry. What made him so sure of himself? She gave him an affronted look and opened her mouth to protest, but the arrival of the waiter put an end to their conversation. Only the knowledge that several of her friends were in the room kept her from getting up and walking out. That would really start tongues wagging! Instead she gritted her teeth and fumed at Miles's arrogance.

As he ordered for both of them, she studied him as unobtrusively as she could. There was more than a hint of ruthlessness about that sensual mouth, and the dark, determined slashes of eyebrow told her he was a man who was used to getting what he wanted.

But not from me, she told him silently and stubbornly. Not from me!

"Are you looking for anything in particular?" Miles asked. His voice was an amused drawl.

Claire flushed. She had been studying him so intently that she hadn't even realized the waiter had gone.

"Don't be embarrassed," he said softly. "I don't mind." He reached over and brushed her cheek with his fingers. It was a gentle caress and shouldn't have sent sparks down the length of her spine. But it did. The table suddenly seemed a little too small, a little too crowded.

Claire fought back the urge to run. The expression on his face was very unnerving.

"I wish you wouldn't look at me like that," she burst out suddenly. Her voice was cross.

"Like what?" He raised his eyebrows questioningly. "I enjoy looking at you as much as you seem to like looking at me."

Claire thought it would be better to ignore his last sentence. "You look at me as though everything I say or do amuses you," she told him irritably.

Miles shook his head. "You don't amuse me," he told her softly. "You intrigue me."

For a moment Claire was tempted to ask why, but her better judgment prevailed. She had a feeling his answer would only unnerve her further, and that was the last thing she needed.

"Do you know what I thought when I first saw you?" he asked. His eyes wandered over her face. "I thought you looked like the perfect southern lady. In that dress you were wearing this afternoon, with your hair pushed back, you looked very prim and proper. But after I had talked to you for a while, I realized that was just a disguise."

"I don't know what you mean," Claire said. A disguise indeed! She gave him an insulted look.

"Don't you?" he asked mildly. "There's a streak of

passion running through you that you try to hide. I can see it in your eyes and in that beautifully shaped mouth of yours. And I can feel it when you talk about your house."

"You're being ridiculous," Claire told him indignantly.

"I don't think so. For now, that house of yours seems to be the center of your life. But when the right man comes along—"

"I suppose you think you're the right man," she interrupted without thinking. Her voice was tart, and her eyes scoffed at him.

A smile touched his lips. It was a smile filled with self-confidence and certainty, and it immediately set her teeth on edge. "Maybe," he said noncommittally.

"Of all the arrogant—" she began.

Before she could tell him exactly what she thought of him, their food arrived. Miles had ordered she-crab soup, laced with sherry and topped with a small mound of whipped cream, and broiled creek flounder. It was exactly what she would have ordered for herself, she thought a little sourly. For some reason, that took a little of the pleasure out of her dinner.

"Tell me about yourself," Miles said as they ate.

Claire gave him an uncertain look. She would have preferred to eat in silence. She suddenly wanted the dinner and the evening to end. Miles was threatening her in a way she didn't quite understand, and she didn't like it.

"What do you want to know?" she asked warily.

"I want to know when you first came to Charleston, how long you've lived here—that kind of thing."

"Why don't we talk about you instead?" she suggested. She definitely did not want to talk about herself. Instinct told her she'd be wise to remain as aloof and inaccessible

44

as possible. Besides, there were things she would like to know about Miles. So far he hadn't been very forthcoming.

His face was momentarily blank. "We can talk about me some other time," he said a little too smoothly.

Claire gave him a sharp look. Most men enjoyed talking about themselves. In fact, that was all some men wanted to do.

"Right now I want to find out about you," he told her, and even though she had warned herself to stay aloof, she couldn't help being flattered by the interest she saw in his face. "Aren't the Ashleys an old Charleston family?" he asked. "There's the Ashley River and Ashley Plantation outside of town."

Claire nodded a little proudly. "There have always been Ashleys in Charleston." At least this was a less personal topic, she told herself comfortingly. She could talk about her ancestors for hours.

"It's a little strange that your father would choose to leave," Miles commented. "All his roots, all his family are here."

Claire shrugged. "I think that's partly why he left. He felt stifled by all the history. He's the kind of man who thrives on the fast pace of modern life."

"And you don't," he said matter-of-factly.

She smiled. "Not really. I suppose I'm a little more old-fashioned than that."

"If you're an example of an old-fashioned woman, then I certainly approve." Before Claire could respond, he went on. "When did you decide to live here?" he wanted to know.

"When I was twelve," Claire told him. She paused, wondering if he was really interested in all this. He certainly seemed to be. His dark eyes were fixed on her encouragingly. "That's when I started spending the summers with my grandmother. I felt as if I'd come home," she said softly. She blushed slightly and cast a doubtful look at Miles. Usually, she didn't like to talk about herself, but Miles seemed so sympathetic and so understanding that the words just slipped out. Much to her surprise, and a little to her dismay, he was surprisingly easy to talk to—when he wanted to be.

"What happened after that?" he asked after a moment.

"You surely aren't interested in hearing my life story?" Claire said a little uncomfortably.

"Oh, but I am," he said at once. He took her hand in his, and Claire immediately felt strength in his long fingers. She knew she should pull her hand away, but she didn't. "I want to know everything about you."

Claire took a deep breath. "Why?" she asked bluntly. This time she did pull her hand from his. His touch was definitely unsettling.

He raised her chin with his finger so that she had to look into his eyes. The intensity of his gaze showed her more than she wanted to see. "Do you really have to ask?" he wanted to know. His voice was soft.

Claire looked away and shrugged. She didn't have to ask, not when he looked at her like that.

Miles leaned forward in his chair. "Look at me," he commanded softly. His voice carried so much quiet authority that Claire did as she was told. His eyes probed hers with disturbing intimacy.

"What are you so afraid of?" he asked. "Is it me?"

"No," she snapped a little angrily. His insistence was beginning to annoy her. "I just don't like the way you're

46

pushing me. If you think you can waltz into my life and sweep me off my feet—"

"You swept me off mine," he interrupted.

Claire gave him a disbelieving look. He didn't seem to her like the kind of man who could be swept off his feet by any woman, let alone her.

"That's ridiculous," she said coldly. "In fact, this entire conversation is ridiculous."

"Then let's go back to what we were talking about before," he said agreeably. "Let's talk about you. When you were twelve, you started spending your summers here. What happened after that?"

Claire sighed again. Oh well, she thought. The story of her life, dull though it might be, was better than the kind of verbal fencing they had just been engaged in. She pushed her plate away. She was no longer hungry. She just wanted to get the evening over with. "After high school, I went to college for a couple of years, then I moved here to stay. My grandmother died a year and a half later and left me the house." She lifted her hands expressively. "That's all there is to it," she said, making her voice light.

"What about your father?" Miles asked. "Wasn't he upset when you inherited the house over his head?"

"No, I don't think so," Claire said thoughtfully. "If anything, he was relieved. You see, our branch of the Ashley family isn't terribly well off. My grandmother left practically nothing but the house. As far as my father was concerned, the house would have been a headache."

"Restoring such an old house is expensive," Miles agreed. "It's a shame your grandmother let it go like that."

Claire flushed at the implied criticism of her grandmother. "It was hardly her fault," she said hotly. "It took all her money just to keep the house from falling into disrepair."

"Why didn't she sell it?"

"Sell it!"

Miles seemed to find the question a perfectly reasonable one, but Claire was horrified.

"She'd never have done that. It's been in the Ashley family since the eighteenth century."

"It would have made her life a lot easier," he pointed out mildly. "She could have moved into a new apartment with all the modern conveniences."

"But she wouldn't have been happy," Claire told him stubbornly. "It wouldn't have been home. It would have broken her heart to see it go out of the family."

"And that's why she left it to you."

Claire nodded. "She knew I loved it as much as she did."

"So you wouldn't sell it, then, either?" he asked. His eyes were intent on her face.

"Never," she told him vehemently. "Never."

"It's obviously far more to you than just a house," he commented. His voice was surprisingly gentle and his dark eyes had grown thoughtful. Claire wished she knew what he was thinking, but he was almost impossible for her to read.

"Far more," she said briefly, and left it at that. Her house meant security and roots to her, the things she had lacked as a child. It was where she belonged.

"I think I'm beginning to understand," he told her.

Claire looked down at the table and didn't answer. She doubted that very much.

"Would you like dessert?" he asked a moment later.

48

She shook her head. Thank goodness, she thought. This very confusing evening was just about over. Who knew what he'd say next? "No, thank you. It's getting late. I think we ought to be going."

Much to her relief, he nodded and motioned for the check.

They walked home in companionable silence, and it relaxed Claire a little. When they reached her house, all was quiet there, too.

"Do you have any brandy?" Miles asked as he took the keys from her hand and opened the door.

She shook her head. "I have some brandy in the kitchen that I use for cooking," she told him. "But that's probably not what you had in mind."

He grimaced. "It's definitely not what I had in mind," he said. "I'll get you some decent brandy tomorrow."

"You don't need to do that," she said at once. "I never drink it."

Miles looked amused. "No, but I do. Since I'm going to be here for two weeks, it won't go to waste."

"Why *are* you staying here?" Claire asked him as he closed the door behind them and handed her the keys. She gave him a direct look. "Wouldn't you be more comfortable in a well-staffed, well-stocked hotel?"

He shook his head. "I don't think so. No matter how hard they try, big hotels lack the personal touch, and the personal touch is what I find so attractive about Ashley House."

Claire stared at him. For a moment his eyes were alive with what she could only call desire. She drew back in confusion.

Miles saw her involuntary movement, and the intensity

in his eyes eased slightly. "If you don't have any brandy," he said easily, "what do you have?"

"I have some Calvados someone gave me for Christmas," she answered reluctantly.

"Good," he replied instantly. "We can take it into the garden. It's too beautiful a night to stay inside."

With a sigh she followed him into the kitchen and watched as he poured the shimmering liquid into two snifters of thin and fragile crystal. He picked up the glasses and carried them outside. Claire trailed along behind him, wishing that he weren't so forceful and wishing, too, that she was less susceptible to his charm.

Once they were outside, her uneasiness increased. It was a warm, starry night, and the only sound they could hear was the tinkling of the small fountain in the center of the lawn. Claire had the feeling that they were the only two people in the world.

Miles led her over to the love seat at the edge of the terrace, sat her down, and handed her one of the glasses.

"What a gorgeous night," Claire murmured as she perched on the edge of the love seat. She looked around the garden with pleasure. It was one of her favorite spots. Her eyes touched the white blooming flowers of the magnolia tree; they seemed almost luminous in the moonlight.

"It is lovely," he agreed. He sat down beside her, and she could feel his large body relaxing. She wished she could relax, too, but the closeness, the sheer masculinity of him, made relaxing impossible.

Casually, his arm slid around her shoulders, and he pulled her against him.

"Miles," she said uncertainly, "I don't think—"

She could almost feel him smile in the darkness. "It's

50

all right," he told her gently. "I won't bite. I just want to touch you, to feel you next to me."

A little reluctantly, Claire let him tighten his arm around her. Short of making a scene and sounding like an inexperienced teen-ager, she didn't know what else to do.

"That isn't so bad, is it?" he asked above her.

Claire didn't answer. A few moments later, she, too, began to relax.

"That's better," he said. Casually, he started stroking her hair.

For Claire, the night was beginning to take on a magical feel. The stars shone a little more brightly, the air caressed her a little more gently. Miles leaned over and lightly touched his lips to hers. For a gentle kiss, it fairly crackled with electricity.

"I've wanted to do this all day," he muttered just before his lips again closed over hers. This was a more intense kiss than the first one, and in response, Claire felt her arms slide around his neck.

When he lifted his lips, Claire opened her eyes. Through the darkness, she could see him smiling at her with tenderness that both surprised and warmed her.

"From the first moment I saw you, I've wanted to take you in my arms and make love to you," he told her in a voice that was growing thicker.

Claire's eyes widened, but only for a moment. His third kiss came swiftly, and when it did, it was devastating. Slowly he coaxed her mouth open and forced her to respond. Claire thought of resisting the pressure of his lips, but only for a moment. The thought whirled away, lost in the velvety darkness of the slow kiss, before she could act upon it.

When their mouths finally separated, Claire was trembling. Miles was trembling, too. This is going too far, too fast, she told herself nervously. She pulled back and began fixing her hair with hands that were none too steady.

"What did you want to talk to me about?" she asked in a desperate attempt to defuse the situation. It was time, she felt, to stop what was happening.

"Hmm . . . ," he murmured interrogatively as he began nibbling at her ear. He wasn't paying much attention to her words. He obviously didn't want to talk.

Claire shivered as his lips moved down her neck. Her pulse was beginning to leap erratically. She had to put an end to this now, before it was too late. She tried to pull away, but Miles was holding her too firmly.

"This afternoon you told me you had something to talk to me about," she said desperately. "What is it?"

"It's nothing important." His voice dismissed her question entirely. "What's important now is us."

"There is no us," Claire said doggedly. She removed her arms from around his neck and sat up as straight as she could. She would have liked to get to her feet, but she wasn't sure her legs would hold her.

"I think there is," he answered. His voice grew deeper and warmer. "Don't you realize that I fell in love with you the moment I walked into your house this afternoon?"

Claire sat in stunned silence for a few seconds, then hurriedly got up and walked over to the fountain. Had he really said what she thought he said? She held out her hand to let the water spill onto it and was horrified to see that it was shaking.

"That's absurd," she said with unnecessary loudness. "There's no such thing as love at first sight."

"Twenty-four hours ago I would have agreed with

you," he said quietly. He got up out of the love seat and followed her over to the fountain. "Now I'm not so sure."

He reached for her, but Claire shook her head and backed away. Nothing like this had ever happened to her before, and she wasn't at all sure how to handle it. It didn't make her feel any better to realize that part of her wanted to accept what he had to say.

Miles jammed his hands into his pants pockets and stared down at her. Even in the darkness, with only the moon and stars for light, he looked formidable—and very attractive, Claire thought. With him looking down at her like that, she was having a hard time holding on to her common sense. She gulped and took another step backward.

"Life isn't like that. Love isn't like that," she whispered. Their conversation seemed to be growing more unreal by the minute. She forced herself to look away from him.

He made a gesture of impatience. "Maybe, maybe not. I can only tell you how I feel." His voice had grown a little curt.

Claire could hardly blame him for sounding impatient. She almost felt sorry for him. He wasn't the kind of man women rejected or refused. "But Miles," she protested, "love has to be nurtured, it has to grow. You can't be in love with me—you don't even know me." She was shaken by the storm of emotions his words were causing.

"I know you in all the ways that count," he told her at once. The urgent tone of his voice brought her eyes up involuntarily. "In a way, I feel as if I've always known you."

Claire stared up at him, and her mouth went dry. She

53

was remembering the way she had felt when they kissed, and for a moment, she wished . . .

Then she pulled herself together. For both their sakes, she had to put an end to this right now.

"I'm flattered, Miles," she said, falling back on a formula she never thought she'd have to use. "You're a charming, attractive man, and any woman—"

He cut her off. "I don't want any woman," he told her ardently. "I only want you." He swept her into his arms and held her close to him.

"Let me go!" Claire immediately protested. She was beginning to be afraid of what he might do next and afraid, too, of how she might respond.

"Relax," Miles said above her. His voice was surprisingly reassuring. "Nothing will happen if you don't want it to. I just want you to feel the magic I feel when our bodies touch."

She did feel it. Even though she didn't want to, she felt it. The swift pounding of her heart frightened her. She wasn't ready for this. Not with Miles, not with any man.

With a surge of strength that surprised both of them, she pushed him away. He caught her arm before she could turn and hurry away.

"Don't run," he murmured. "It won't do any good. If you won't let me hold you, let's sit down and talk instead."

"I don't have anything to say," she told him.

But he led her back over to the terrace and gently pushed her into a chair. He sat down across from her, took her hand, and linked her fingers with his.

"You may not," he answered, "but I do. I just told you I love you. Doesn't that mean anything to you?"

Claire thought she heard something in his voice that

touched her. He was hurt by the way she was behaving, and she couldn't blame him. She hadn't been very gracious.

"Of course it does," she said gently, "but . . ." Her voice trailed off and she had to begin again. "All right, Miles. Just for the sake of discussion, let's say I did fall in love with you. You're only here for two weeks. What happens after that? Do you just pack up and leave me with a broken heart?"

"Of course not," he said. He sounded genuinely shocked at the thought. "You'd come with me."

"But Charleston is my home," she told him. "I don't want to leave it."

"Then we'd work something out," he said. He was getting impatient again. "You're talking about minor details—"

"They aren't minor to me," she put in tartly.

"—because you're afraid to face the truth."

"And what is the truth?" she asked with a sigh. Reasoning with him obviously wasn't going to work.

"The truth is that we belong together," he said with quiet assurance. "I know it, and deep down inside, I think you know it, too."

"I don't know anything of the sort!" she exclaimed in frustration.

"Then I'll prove it to you." He got up suddenly and pulled her to her feet. At the touch of his hands on her bare arms, the ground seemed to tremble a little beneath her feet.

"What do you feel when I touch you?" he demanded roughly. His hands began to move with a tantalizing slowness up and down her arms. "What does your heart tell you when we kiss?"

55

Claire opened her mouth to reply, but Miles fastened his lips to hers before she had a chance to say anything. It was a powerful kiss, and though Claire tried her best not to respond to it, she could feel her body inclining toward his.

"You can't pretend you didn't feel anything," he told her triumphantly a minute later. "The look on your face and the way you kissed me back tell me differently."

Claire shook her head. "You're talking about a purely physical reaction," she said. She wished her voice were more steady and her breathing more regular. It would have made her words sound more convincing. "There's a lot more to love than that."

"Of course there is," he agreed irritably. "But the feelings we share when we touch are important, too. I'd like to take you up to my bedroom right now and show you just how important they are. Imagine the two of us together in that big old bed," he urged her in low, sensuous tones. His dark, passionate eyes captured hers and began probing them intently. "Imagine the two of us making love."

"I won't!" Claire cried. Somehow she managed to wrench free. Her body was suddenly trembling, and her legs refused to support her. No matter how hard she tried to ignore his words, she couldn't help visualizing the two of them locked in an intimate embrace. The vision was more than she could bear. She sank back down into the chair behind her. "I think you'd better leave my house first thing tomorrow morning," she said dully. "One of the hotels in town will put you up."

His eyebrows rose. "I have no intention of leaving."

Claire didn't know what to say. He dropped down into

the chair across from her and took her hands in his once again.

"I've been going too fast for you," he said ruefully. "No wonder you're confused. It's just that I've never been particularly patient. I've never had to be. When I see what I want, I go after it."

Claire could believe that.

"It's so obvious to me that we belong together," he went on, "that it seems a shame to wait for anything."

She got to her feet and walked past him. This time he didn't try to stop her.

"Think about what I've said," he urged her. "Maybe by morning you'll begin to realize that I'm right."

She didn't answer. She couldn't. She was past speech. Instead, she went into the house and left him standing by himself in the garden.

CHAPTER THREE

Claire was awake long before her alarm went off. She had tossed and turned most of the night, thinking about Miles. To say that she was confused was something of an understatement. To begin with, she was upset by the way she felt about him. Much as she hated to admit it, she was actually attracted to this brash, arrogant, rather alarming man who had stormed into her home and her life and had tried his best to bowl her over.

All she wanted out of life, all she had ever wanted, was stability and emotional security. Once she moved to Charleston, she had promised herself there would be no more wrenching good-byes. And now she found herself close to falling for a man who claimed he was in love with her after only a few brief hours. Every bit of common sense Claire possessed told her that this was no basis for a lasting relationship.

It was like something out of a fairy tale, she mused as she got dressed. Attractive, dynamic men like Miles Sinclair simply did not fall in love with bed and breakfast proprietors at the drop of a hat.

He came down to breakfast at eight forty-five, joined the schoolteachers, and spent the entire meal entertaining them with stories of his travels. He was pleasant to

Claire, but not familiar, and as she poured his coffee, she couldn't help wondering if she had really stood in his arms last night and listened to him say he wanted to make love to her. The whole thing was growing more and more dreamlike in her memory.

At the end of the meal, however, he lingered long enough to ask if he could see her later in the morning. Claire felt her heart rebound as she nodded, and she had to turn away so he wouldn't see the happiness in her eyes. Perhaps she hadn't imagined last night after all, she thought happily as she hurried into the kitchen.

When she came back into the kitchen, she found Sarah sitting at the small, round table in the middle of the room munching on a piece of toast.

"Good morning," Claire said. "Where'd you come from?"

"I came in the back way," Sarah answered. "I didn't want to disturb your guests. Don't you ever lock your door?"

"Only at night," Claire told her mildly as she started filling the dishwasher with dishes. "What are you doing here so early?"

Sarah looked surprised. "I want to talk to you about last night, of course," she said. "Stop fiddling with those dishes and come over here and sit down. This is important."

Obediently, Claire dried her hands and sat down in one of the other chairs. Sarah *had* looked a bit strange last night, she reminded herself. Maybe there was more to it than the fact that she had seen Claire out with a handsome man.

"I don't understand," Sarah began. Her voice changed as she got a good look at her friend. "Claire," she exclaimed. "You look terrible. Are you sick?" There were delicate shadows under Claire's eyes, and her face was pale.

"I'm all right," Claire replied shortly.

She had no intention of telling Sarah what had happened the night before or how it had kept her awake most of the night. Sarah would just laugh and say Claire was making a mountain out of a molehill. No man would ever keep Sarah awake worrying, Claire thought. Sarah's love life was important to her but not as important as her beauty sleep.

"I didn't sleep well, that's all," she added, trying to sound a little less abrupt.

"It's that man," Sarah said, going to the heart of the matter. "I want to know what he did to you."

"He didn't do anything," Claire replied. "We had dinner together. That's all."

Sarah looked at her critically. "Well, something must have happened to make you look like that."

"Nothing happened," Claire repeated, a little less patiently this time.

Her friend sighed. "I don't understand what you were doing having dinner with that man anyway. I can't believe you've gone over to the enemy."

"And I don't have the faintest idea what you're talking about," she said. "Miles Sinclair is a guest here. What do you mean by saying he's the enemy?"

It was Sarah's turn to look surprised. "He's staying *here?*" she echoed. "I don't believe it!"

"Why not?" Claire asked. "He's staying in the Blue Room."

Sarah shook her head. "Some people have all the nerve," she commented. There was a kind of reluctant

60

admiration in her voice. Then the expression on her face changed. "Don't you know who Miles Sinclair is?"

Claire shook her head. "He told me he was a tourist from Chicago. That's all I know."

"And you believed him?" Sarah sounded incredulous.

"Of course I believed him," Claire said defensively. "Why shouldn't I?"

"Does he look like a typical tourist?" Sarah wanted to know.

"Well, no," Claire replied slowly, "he doesn't. But that doesn't mean . . ."

Sarah stared at her friend in exasperation. "Honestly, Claire, you can be so naïve at times. Miles Sinclair is the hotel man I was telling you about. He's the man I saw in Michael's office!"

Claire's face, pale already from lack of sleep, lost its remaining color. Suddenly everything fell into place. Miles Sinclair! She knew now why his name sounded so familiar. Miles Sinclair *was* Hotels Americana, the chain of sleek luxury hotels that, over the past ten years, had sprung up in every major city.

"He's the man—" Claire began weakly.

"—who wants to buy several houses, including yours, so he can put up one of his fancy hotels," Sarah finished for her.

"I don't believe it!" Claire said loudly. If Sarah was telling the truth, it meant . . . she didn't want to think what it meant.

"Why don't you believe it?" Sarah asked.

"Because—because he didn't say a thing about a hotel to me," Claire told her lamely.

"Well, you'd better believe it," Sarah said grimly. "He's already approached the Bowens. It looks as if

61

you're next on the list. Why else would he be so interested?"

Why else, indeed? Claire thought. Anger was growing deep inside her. What had he told her? she asked herself. That he was in construction? Not a lie, exactly—but not exactly the truth, either. And what about the other things he had said last night? They probably weren't true, either.

She shook her head, trying to clear it a little. She was so angry, she was having a hard time thinking straight. "He was so nice," she said numbly.

Sarah laughed sharply. "I'll bet he was. He was softening you up," she told her friend callously. "That's why he took you to dinner. He was using psychological warfare. I've met men like him before. He'd say or do anything to get what he wanted."

Claire winced. Sarah was right. Miles was obviously an unprincipled, unethical businessman who didn't mind using whoever got in his way. And to think she had believed him! she thought with horror.

"What I don't understand is why he hasn't offered to buy your house," Sarah pursued. "Last night would have been the perfect opportunity."

"He didn't say anything about it," she said shortly.

All his compliments, she was thinking furiously, all his words of love at first sight had been nothing more than a carefully concocted plan to get hold of her property. He must have thought she was very gullible. And he was right, she thought even more furiously. She had been gullible enough to believe him!

"What an idiot I've been," she said aloud. "I should have known better."

Sarah gave her a sharp look. "Claire," she said, concern suddenly softening her voice. "Last night . . . nothing happened, did it?"

"Of course not," Claire said, giving Sarah a clear, slightly affronted look. "I'm not that much of an idiot."

Sarah hesitated for a moment. "Well, then, have you fallen for him?"

"Fallen for that—for that—" Claire couldn't think of words strong enough to describe him. "No," she said with finality. "I haven't fallen for him. Besides, you know that the last thing I want to do is get involved with someone."

"I'm sorry," Sarah said apologetically. "I had to ask. He's extraordinarily good looking, and if I know men, he's got charm to go with those looks. It would complicate things if you had fallen for him," she added, "and I don't want to see you hurt."

"Well, you can stop worrying. I could never fall for a man like that."

Sarah gave Claire another sharp look, then gazed at her silently for a moment. "Good," she said finally. "I'm glad to hear that. Now what are we going to do?"

"The first thing I'm going to do is tell him to leave my house," Claire said grimly. "Then I'm going to tell him exactly what I think of him. By the end of the day, he'll be on his way back to Chicago."

"I wouldn't be too sure of that," Sarah warned her. "He's not the type to give up easily. If he can't get your house, he'll probably try to buy someone else's. Michael says he's very determined."

"We've got to stop him," Claire said vehemently. "He'll ruin Charleston if he has his way."

"We'll stop him," Sarah said. "As a matter of fact, I've got a plan."

"Good," Claire said. "I'm certainly willing to do my part to see that he doesn't succeed."

"I'm glad to hear that," Sarah said a little dryly, "because this plan depends on you."

"On me?" Claire asked, startled.

"On you," Sarah said firmly. "I don't think throwing Miles Sinclair out of your house is the right way to handle this," she went on.

"After what he's done—" Claire began in outraged tones.

"Oh, he deserves it—and more," Sarah agreed. "But in this case I think it might be wiser to let him stay where he is."

"Why?" Claire wanted to know. She couldn't believe what she was hearing.

"He's not the kind of man who gives up easily," Sarah told her. "If you kick him out, he'll just move into a hotel and continue trying to buy property from there. But if he stays with you, you'll be able to keep tabs on him."

"I don't see how," Claire objected. "Just because he's staying here doesn't mean he'll tell me anything."

"You'll have to make him tell you," Sarah said simply.

"*Make* him tell me?" Claire echoed incredulously. "Just how am I supposed to do that?"

Sarah sighed. "I was hoping I wouldn't have to spell this out for you. It seems so obvious to me." Her voice grew persuasive. "I saw the way he looked at you last night. The man definitely finds you attractive. You can use the way he feels to get him to tell you what you want to know. Think of yourself as a spy in the enemy's camp," she finished brightly.

"It won't work," Claire said at once. "In the first

place, he's not attracted to me—he's attracted to my house."

"I think you're wrong about that," Sarah told her quickly. "I know what I saw, and last night I definitely saw a man who was interested."

Claire ignored her. "And in the second place, he'd never tell me anything, even if he were interested in me."

"You'll have to work at it, of course," Sarah said thoughtfully. "You'll have to flatter him and play up to him and seduce him—"

Claire winced. "Now wait just a minute," she began.

"—into telling you what you want to know," Sarah finished calmly.

"I can't do that," Claire objected. She didn't want to do it, she told herself. She never wanted to see Miles Sinclair again. "I'm not that good an actress. Besides, it's a sneaky, underhanded thing to do."

"I know," Sarah said with satisfaction. "That's the beauty of it. No one would ever suspect *you* of anything sneaky or underhanded. It's a foolproof plan. He'll never know what hit him."

"I don't like it," Claire said uneasily. That was an understatement. If she did what Sarah was suggesting, it meant she'd have to spend time with Miles—a lot of time. She'd already seen how dangerous that could be.

Sarah seemed to know what she was thinking. "Is there something you're not telling me?" she asked.

"No, of course not," Claire replied a little too quickly. "It's just that the whole thing seems a little unfair."

"He deserves it," her friend said. "Didn't he try to trick you? Besides, it's not as if you're doing this for yourself," she added guilelessly. "You're doing it for Charleston."

"I suppose I could take him around the city and show him why Charleston is so special," Claire said slowly. She still didn't like the idea, but Sarah was right. He did deserve it, and more.

"That's a wonderful idea," Sarah said enthusiastically. "You can start tomorrow night. I'm sure your cousin won't mind if you bring Miles to the Fancy Dress Ball."

"I don't know," Claire said reluctantly. "I'll have to think about it."

"There's really nothing to think about," Sarah told her. "You can't back out." She paused. "I'm counting on you and Charleston's counting on you."

That brought a smile to Claire's lips. Sarah loved to dramatize.

"Miles Sinclair is no General Sherman," she said dryly. "He's talking about building a hotel, not destroying the city."

"It's practically the same thing," Sarah said airily. Her voice changed. "I'm not asking you to sleep with him, for heaven's sake. I'm just suggesting that you play up to him a little. You know what my grandmother always said. You can catch more flies with honey than vinegar."

Claire shuddered. She had never liked that expression.

"I'll think about it," she said again.

"I knew we could count on you," Sarah said triumphantly. "Just let me know the minute you find out something. Once we know what he's going to do, Michael will find a way to stop him." She glanced down at her watch, and her eyes widened. "I've got to go. See you tomorrow night."

Could she beat Miles at his own game? Claire wondered as she stared at the door Sarah had just closed. Every instinct she possessed told her to stay away from him. In less than twenty-four hours, he had already come close to turning her life upside down. What would happen if she actually encouraged him?

Nothing, she told herself firmly. Nothing would happen now that she knew what he was really like.

Besides, she thought again with a little spirit of contemptuous anger, Sarah was right. He deserved whatever he got. He had tried to deceive her, after all. It probably wouldn't hurt him to be on the receiving end of a little underhanded treatment for a while.

She finished cleaning up the breakfast dishes and went out to her desk in the hall, hoping some work on her plans for the third floor would take her mind off Miles. She was sitting there, trying her best not to think of him, when he came down the stairs.

"Hi," he said softly as he approached her desk. "I'm glad to see you're alone. I want to talk to you."

Claire looked up, and for a few heart-stopping seconds, the warmth in his eyes took her straight back to the night before. Horrified, she reminded herself of how angry she was with him.

"And I want to talk to you," she said, trying to sound friendlier than she felt. It wasn't easy. "My cousin is holding his annual Fancy Dress Ball tomorrow night. I thought you might like to go with me."

"I'd like that very much," he said with a smile of dizzying warmth. "What about dinner tonight? We could pick up where we left off last night."

Before she could stop herself, Claire gave him an incredulous look. The nerve of the man! He was still determined to use her to get what he wanted.

Then she clamped down hard on her emotions. He didn't know that she had learned of his plans. For the moment, at least, that gave her the upper hand. She forced herself to relax a little.

"I can't have dinner with you tonight," she said, trying to sound regretful. Spy or no spy, she had to have some time to herself to get her thoughts in order. She had accepted her role, but she wasn't sure how to play it.

"Why not?" he wanted to know.

"Because I promised to have dinner with someone else," she said coolly. She was annoyed with the way he was pressing her.

He gave her a probing glance. "Is something wrong?" he asked. "You look a little strange."

"Nothing is wrong," she replied quickly. She wasn't doing a very good job of hiding her feelings, she thought a little ruefully. She hesitated a moment, then took a deep breath. "Miles," she said quietly, "there's a rumor going around that you're here in Charleston to find a spot to put up a big hotel. Is that true?" She told herself she was a fool for asking, for even hoping that he'd deny it.

He didn't deny it, but he didn't confirm it, either.

He shrugged noncommittally. "Perhaps. I haven't really decided what I want to do," he said a little vaguely.

Claire's heart sank. It *was* true. He *was* after her house.

"But that's got nothing to do with us," he told her. He walked around the desk and lifted her out of her chair. She felt like a rag doll in his arms. His voice dropped, and his eyes grew even warmer. "I meant what I said last night. From the moment I walked through your door, I knew you were someone very special. Before you even said anything, I wanted to take you in my arms. I wanted to hold you and kiss you."

As Claire gazed up at him, the floor seemed to tilt slightly. Then she hardened her heart. Miles was obviously going to go ahead with his plan. He was leaving her no choice but to go ahead with hers.

"We could have something very special," he murmured as his lips moved closer to hers, "and we both know it."

Claire pulled away. She had to admit he was persuasive, very persuasive. Angry though she was, she recognized that.

"I have a million things to do," she said a little breathlessly.

He reached out and touched her hair gently. "All right," he said. "I'll let you go—for now."

He went back up the stairs, and Claire sank down into her chair and pushed her hands through her hair. In spite of everything she knew, she still found him attractive. It was a disconcerting thought.

I'm going to have to do a better job than that, she told herself, if I'm going to learn anything. She obviously wasn't cut out to be a spy.

69

CHAPTER FOUR

There's no reason to be nervous about tonight, Claire told herself over and over again as she slipped into the pale blue watered-silk gown she had found packed away in a trunk in the attic. Now that she knew what Miles was really like, there was nothing he could say or do that would have any effect on her at all.

She glanced in the mirror, and her eyes widened. For a moment, she hadn't recognized herself. In the old-fashioned dress, with its panniered skirt over rustling petticoats, she looked as if she had just stepped out of the pages of history. Layers of creamy white, intricately handworked lace were covered by watered silk in a color so beautiful, it took her breath away. An iridescent aqua, it could be blue or green, depending on the light.

She frowned as she focused on the neckline. It was a little too décolleté for her taste, but no amount of pulling or tugging would make it cover the creamy curve of her breasts any more than it already did.

She sighed. She wasn't looking forward to the look on Miles's face when he saw her, but there was nothing she could do about it now. That's what she got for waiting till the last moment to decide what to wear, she told herself a little crossly. As it was, she'd been very lucky to find this dress. It was a good thing for her that the Ashleys never threw anything away.

She glanced at the clock, picked up a shawl and fan—more dividends of her search in the attic—and hurried down to the first floor. She wasn't going to descend the stairs under the scrutiny of Miles's eyes, as she had before. Tonight she was going to be waiting for him!

When Miles finally joined her in the hall, she nearly gasped. He was dressed totally in black, except for his white, slightly ruffled shirt. He looked alarmingly masculine and devilishly handsome. He swept her a low, courtly bow, and Claire couldn't help dropping into a deep curtsy in return.

"If I had a moustache, I'd twirl it," he told her. "What do you think of this riverboat gambler getup?"

"It's very effective," Claire murmured. Her blue eyes suddenly danced with amusement. "And very appropriate."

He gave her a slow smile and a wink. "Do you think so? As a matter of fact," he told her in a voice that brought a faint stain of pink to her cheeks, "when it comes to my personal life, I only gamble on sure things."

"And I suppose you consider me a sure thing?" she asked tartly. She was nettled, and she let him know it.

He shrugged. "You said it," he told her, "I didn't."

As he spoke, his gaze wandered over her body. Approval warmed his eyes. Just as Claire had expected, his eyes stopped briefly and appreciatively at the spot where her dress met her bare skin. Claire felt herself tense, and the pink grew deeper in her cheeks. She stared back at him as if defying him to say anything.

"What a wonderful copy of a pre–Civil War ball gown," he commented in a fairly impersonal voice. He seemed to realize that a personal comment would not go over well at the moment.

Claire relaxed slightly. "It's not a copy," she said. "It's the real thing. I found it in the attic."

"It must be close to 125 years old!" he exclaimed. "Turn around so I can see it."

Claire pivoted slowly. She couldn't help being aware of how graceful the dress made her look as she turned.

"Beautiful," he murmured softly when she had finished. "Just beautiful."

The personal note was back in his voice, and she couldn't tell whether he was talking about the dress or her.

"If I had known what you were going to wear, I'd have arranged to have one of those carriages I keep seeing down by the market drive us to your cousin's home. It would be much more appropriate than a car."

Claire shook her head. "It would take us forever to get there in a carriage," she said coolly. "A car is far more practical."

"But not nearly as romantic," he murmured.

She started to tell him that romance was the last thing on her mind, but she stopped herself. That was no way to put her plan into operation.

"Shall we go?" she asked instead, forcing herself to smile up at him.

He took her arm and led her outside to the car. Then he opened the car door and settled her into the seat. In a gesture that was a little too intimate and that brought their lips just a little too close together, he fastened the seat belt around her.

"I can do that for myself," Claire told him. She was almost afraid to move.

"Of course you can," he answered. "But isn't it nicer when I do it?"

He turned his head slightly, and his lips just grazed hers as he pulled back. It was the briefest of kisses, as well as the lightest, but it took Claire's breath away. She immediately looked down and began fiddling with the seat belt so that he couldn't see the expression on her face. When he got into the car, she told him how to get to her cousin's in offhand tones, then lapsed into silence. She wasn't going to let him know what his touch, his very closeness, did to her.

"I take it the Fancy Dress Ball is an annual event," Miles said after a while.

Claire nodded. "Like most everything else around here, it has its roots in history. Before the Civil War, a ball was always held at Ashley Plantation this time of year. Only in those days, it was more than a ball. It was like an all-day party. People started arriving in the morning, then there was a barbecue, and at night there was dancing."

"It sounds like quite a celebration," he commented.

"It was. These days, of course, that kind of lavish entertaining is almost impossible. But about ten years ago, my cousin decided to revive the ball. This is only the second time I've attended," she added, and immediately wondered why she had told him that.

"You don't go out much," he said. It was more of a statement than a question.

"No," she said briefly, and left it at that.

Miles was silent for a moment. He seemed to be thinking about something. "Then it's not just me," he said finally. "I was beginning to wonder."

"What's not just you?" she asked suspiciously. She had a feeling she was going to be sorry she asked.

He turned his head and gave her a serious look. "It's not just me you're afraid of being involved with. It's all men, isn't it?"

Claire stared straight ahead of her. "You don't know what you're talking about," she told him in chilly tones.

"Don't I?" he asked. "Then why don't you go out more often? You're a beautiful woman. It can't be because of a lack of invitations."

"I don't go out much because I don't have the time," Claire told him. Her voice was even more chilly than before. "Not that it's any of your business."

"It *is* my business," he said ominously. Then he smiled. "At least I don't have to worry about the competition."

"Turn left at the next road," Claire told him. This was a topic she definitely didn't want to pursue. "Then go about two miles and take the next right. That's the driveway."

Miles followed her instructions without comment, and in a few moments they were traveling down a long, tree-lined drive with moss-draped oaks, which brought them to the front of Ashley Plantation.

The old plantation house looked festive and welcoming. Light streamed from all the windows, and her cousin, David, and his wife, Anne, were standing on the wide veranda greeting their guests. Inside, the atmosphere was more festive still. Guests in beautiful costumes stood laughing and talking while waiters circulated with trays of champagne.

Slowly they made their way into the ballroom, stopping and speaking to everyone Claire knew. As she had

74

predicted, Miles's presence created quite a stir. Everyone —all the women at least—wanted to meet him, and Claire found herself performing introductions over and over again. Once they reached the ballroom, Miles was taken from her by a woman who "just knew Claire wouldn't mind if she borrowed her escort for a few minutes."

As soon as Miles disappeared, Sarah materialized by her side.

"You look wonderful," Sarah said. She gave Claire an admiring glance.

Claire turned to her. "You're the one who looks wonderful," she replied, admiring her friend in her brilliant emerald green gown with a very provocative neckline. Sarah was the perfect southern belle.

Sarah waved away the compliment. "I see you brought him," she said in a lowered voice. "I have to admit he looks pretty good." She stared at him critically as he whirled by them. He was dancing with a woman who was hanging onto his every word with flattering interest. "He'll be the hit of the ball," she added a little glumly.

Claire shrugged. "That might be all for the good," she pointed out.

"I suppose so," Sarah agreed without any noticeable enthusiasm. "I just hate to see someone like that having a good time." Her voice brightened. "Have you found out anything yet?" she asked eagerly.

"Well, hardly," Claire replied dryly. "I haven't had enough time. Besides, I don't think this is going to work. Miles is too shrewd a businessman to blurt out his plans."

"That's why you have to worm the information out of him," Sarah told her. "Use your feminine wiles. Make him think he's irresistible."

"He already thinks that," Claire said shortly.

"Does he? Good. Then your work's half done. Don't get squeamish now," Sarah cautioned her friend. "There's too much at stake."

And you only know part of it, Claire sighed to herself as she reminded herself of the way he had tried to use her. "You're right," she said a little unhappily. "It's just that I'm not cut out for this Mata Hari stuff."

Miles danced by them with still another woman in his arms. Claire tried not to stare, but she couldn't help being a little annoyed. Miles was supposed to be her escort, but since they had arrived she had seen practically nothing of him.

"You'd better dance with someone else," Sarah told her. She, too, was watching Miles. "It looks as if you're not going to see much of him this evening."

"I might as well have stayed at home," Claire grumbled. "This evening's going to be a complete waste of time." She was shocked to find that jealousy, the green-eyed monster, was lurking somewhere deep inside her. She tried to tell herself that she *couldn't* be jealous of those women in Miles's arms, but the fact remained that she was.

"Nonsense," Sarah said briskly. "Since you're here, you're going to have a good time. I'm going to see to that."

Sarah's words brought a faint smile to Claire's face. "All right," she said with resignation. "What do I do?"

"You leave that to me," her friend said. "In a moment you'll have so many partners, you won't know what to do with them."

Sarah was as good as her word. Before Claire quite

knew what was happening, she was out on the dance floor.

She would have enjoyed herself if it hadn't been for Miles. Occasionally, he got close enough to give her a warm smile, but for the most part they were separated by a sea of bodies. Claire tried to forget that he was somewhere on the dance floor. When that didn't work, she tried to tell herself that she had brought him to the ball for strictly impersonal reasons. Neither ploy worked. She couldn't help it. She wanted to dance with him; she wanted to feel his arms around her.

She was halfway through her third dance when Miles cut in.

"Hello, stranger," he told her as he slid an arm around her waist and began dancing her toward the edge of the dance floor. "Every time I've seen you, you've been with a different man. And to think I said I wouldn't have to worry about the competition!" he added ruefully.

"You haven't been doing so badly yourself," she pointed out. "You must have danced with every woman here."

"It feels like it," he agreed at once. "Why didn't you come rescue me?"

"You didn't look as if you needed rescuing," Claire said. "You looked as if you were having a good time."

"Is that jealousy I see in those beautiful blue eyes of yours?" he asked.

"It most certainly is not!" she replied indignantly.

"You don't need to be jealous," he went on exactly as if she hadn't said a thing. "I was only being polite."

"I'm not jealous," she repeated a little heatedly.

"Well, I don't mind admitting that I'm jealous of the men you were dancing with," he said. "In fact, I have no intention of letting you dance with anyone but me for the rest of the evening."

"Just how are you going to manage that?" Claire asked skeptically.

"Very easily," he said with a twinkle in his eyes. "Just watch this."

Two more steps and an expert twirl brought them up to the French doors leading to the wide, brick terrace. A moment later, they were through the doors. They weren't alone, though. Other couples had discovered that it was cooler outside.

Miles led Claire to a secluded corner of the terrace where they could dance unseen by anyone else. It wasn't a big space, but it was enough. Tall shrubs blocked it from view.

"We can be alone here," Miles said simply as he pulled her back into his arms.

Claire had come reluctantly. She wasn't sure she should be alone with him.

She looked over his shoulder and saw an elaborate iron table and chair. On the table were an ice bucket, complete with a bottle of chilling champagne, and two glasses.

"We can't stay here," she said at once. "David must be planning on using this part of the terrace for something."

Miles pulled back a little and gave her a questioning look.

"I put those there," he said when he saw what she was looking at. "I thought we deserved a private little celebration of our own." His arms tightened around her. "Now relax and enjoy yourself."

"I can't," she said miserably. The truth was that she was afraid to relax. She was afraid to enjoy herself. She was afraid of where it would lead. "We should be going back inside. People will wonder what happened to us."

"Nobody in that crowd will miss us," he said imperturbably. "But I do think you're right about one thing. We need to find someplace else to be alone."

Miles suddenly let go of her, and for a brief second, Claire felt a sense of loss. Without his arms around her, the night was suddenly cold. Then she noticed what he was doing. He stuck the champagne bottle under his arm, picked up the two glasses and held them in his long, tapered fingers, then took her arm with his other hand.

"Come on," he said urgently. "Let's find someplace more private."

Without giving her a chance to say anything, he pulled her down the steps and across the lawn at such a pace that Claire, her skirt billowing behind her, had to run to keep up with him. She had no choice. His hand was steely hard around her arm as she flew along beside him.

"Where are we going?" she asked him a little angrily.

He looked down at her, and his pace slowed a little. "I don't know," he confessed. Still holding her by the arm, he began to move down a garden path. "We'll just wander around until we find a good spot to drink our champagne."

"This is ridiculous," Claire told him crossly.

He turned to face her. His eyes were warm and persuasive in the moonlight. "Humor me," he murmured. "I just want to be alone with you, completely alone for a few minutes. We'll have a glass of champagne, and then, if you want to go back to the house, we will. I'm not going to hold you anywhere against your will."

"Why not?" she asked immediately. "You're already bringing me here against my will."

"Am I?" he asked softly. He let go of her arm, and his eyes probed hers a little more deeply.

"No," she whispered after a long, intense moment. "I suppose you're not." She detached her eyes with difficulty. "There's a summer house down near the river. I don't think anyone else will venture that far."

"It sounds perfect," he murmured.

"But we're only going to stay for one glass of champagne," she cautioned him.

"Whatever you say," he promised. "Though I'll do my best to change your mind."

"I'm sure you will," Claire answered dryly. She knew she should lead him someplace where there were bright lights and lots of people, but she didn't. Instead, she led him deeper into the grounds. Hand in hand, they crossed a small white fretwork bridge that spanned a dry stream bed and disappeared into the darkness.

"How many other lovers do you suppose have walked beneath the trees?" Miles asked.

"We aren't lovers," she protested breathlessly.

"Not yet," he told her in a voice that was low and husky.

"Not ever," she told him more breathlessly still. Not even she thought she sounded vehement in her denial.

"Not yet," he repeated imperturbably. "But we will be —and soon. I told you before, I don't like waiting."

"And I don't like being pushed," she retorted. Good, she thought as she heard her words. She sounded more like her usual self.

"I'm not pushing," Miles told her. His hand tightened around hers. "Just encouraging."

"There's the summer house," she said unnecessarily. It rose white and almost ghostlike in the moonlight. Still

80

hand in hand, they walked inside. Claire sat on one of the banquettes that lined the walls and watched Miles as he expertly opened the bottle of champagne and splashed a little into the glasses.

"To us," he said meaningfully as he touched his glass to hers.

Claire looked into his face then took a gulp of the bubbling wine. It tickled all the way down her throat. The setting was too romantic, and Miles was gazing at her too warmly for her to be angry at his insinuation.

"Would you like to dance?" he asked. He held out his arms.

"There's no music," she protested. Her protest was halfhearted, and they both knew it. She suddenly wanted to be back in his arms.

"We'll make our own music," he told her with the self-assured smile that she normally found irritating. At this moment it didn't seem to bother her.

She rose with a graceful motion and stepped into his arms. Both his hands went around her waist, and after a moment's hesitation she wrapped her arms around his neck and rested her head against his shoulder.

"Can you hear it?" he asked as they swayed back and forth together in a close embrace.

She shook her head. "All I can hear is the beating of your heart." It was true. His heart beat so steadily and so loudly beneath her head that it drowned out the sound of everything else.

"Some people, most people, go through life without experiencing anything like this," Miles told her.

Claire could easily believe that. She had come out to the summer house intending to have one glass of champagne. But now time seemed to have stopped. She just wanted to enjoy the feel of his body against hers and the clean, masculine scent of him as she breathed in the balmy night air.

He bent his head and fastened his lips to hers. Claire felt a thrill run down her spine. She tilted her head back and let him kiss her.

"We ought to make the most of moments like these," he murmured when their lips finally parted. As he gazed down at her, the look in his eyes deepened. "Let me make love to you," he urged her.

Before she could answer, he again claimed her lips. The kindness and gentleness were still there, but passion now had the upper hand. His mouth was insistent, and so were his hands. Before Claire knew it, they were leading her down a path she didn't want to travel.

"We can't make love here," she told him unsteadily when she was finally able to speak. His lips were tracing a lazy path down her neck. Claire felt herself tremble as they went lower and lower. She was beginning to have trouble with her breathing. "Anyone could come out here and find us," she gasped.

He dismissed her objection with a wave of the hand. "No one is going to come all the way out here."

"Why not?" she countered. "We did."

He ignored her words, pulling her over to the banquette and sitting down. He held Claire close to him, so close that she felt a little trapped.

"My dress!" she whispered as his hands slid the gown from her shoulders. She had to put a stop to this—now! She wasn't going to let him make love to her just so she could find out his plans.

He misunderstood. "I can manage your dress," he assured her as the dress slid farther and farther down her arms.

"Miles!" she cried out. "Stop!"

Miles stopped, but she could tell he was getting angry.

"What is all this?" he demanded sharply. "Why are you suddenly stopping me?"

"Because I don't want to make love," she answered miserably. "I've been trying to tell you—"

"You haven't been trying very hard," he broke in angrily.

"—but you wouldn't listen," she finished. She moved away from him and gently tugged the sleeves of her dress back where they belonged. It wasn't easy, the way her hands were shaking.

He watched her in silence, but only for a minute. "I'll help you with that," he told her. The impatience was gone from his voice.

Claire stepped back as he came toward her. "I can do it myself," she told him in a voice that wasn't as firm as she would have liked it to be.

"Don't be silly," he said. "You might tear it." Slowly and carefully, he adjusted her dress. When it was back in place, he cupped her chin in his hand and brought her head up so that she had to look at him.

"So you don't want to make love?" he asked in a conversational voice. For all its pleasantness, his voice had a steely undercurrent to it.

"No," she answered. She faced him with what she hoped was a cool, steady gaze.

"Try telling your body that," he murmured. He bent his head. "It was sending out signals no man could ignore. I certainly couldn't ignore them. Shall I show you all over again?"

"No!" Claire cried. She jerked her chin from his hand and moved away. He was standing between her and the door, so she couldn't have run even if she had wanted to. And she didn't want to, she told herself firmly. She wasn't afraid of him.

"What about the way your body responds when I touch you?" he wanted to know.

"It's a purely physical reaction," Claire insisted. "I've told you that before. It doesn't mean anything."

"It means something to me," he told her. He picked up their forgotten champagne glasses and refilled them. He handed one to Claire, and she sipped at it gratefully. Her knees were so unsteady, she would have liked to sit down. But she was afraid Miles would take that as a sign of weakness—or worse.

"What about one last dance before we leave?"

Claire shook her head. She didn't want Miles to touch her again. It was too dangerous; he was too dangerous to her peace of mind.

His voice turned a little mocking. "Surely you're not going to deny me one last dance?" he asked. The look on his face made her feel a little foolish. Was it her imagination, or was there suppressed amusement in his eyes?

"Not if that's all it is," she answered primly.

"That's all," he promised.

As he pulled her back into his arms, she had the uncomfortable feeling that he was laughing at her. She suddenly felt young and inexperienced. Neither was a pleasant feeling.

Together they whirled around and around the summer

house to the accompaniment of the frogs and crickets and the wind sighing in the trees. Claire tried not to relax against him, tried to remind herself that she was here to win him over, not the other way around.

CHAPTER FIVE

Claire sank gratefully down onto one of the benches in the White Point Gardens and stared out at the ocean. It was a view she never grew tired of, though she was tired enough today. She and Miles had been on their feet since morning, walking around historic Charleston, taking in every site she felt could possibly interest him, from St. Michael's Church to the historically nonexistent "Catfish Row," made famous by Gershwin's folk opera *Porgy and Bess*. As they walked around the city, looking at the graceful pastel houses, Claire sprinkled her guided tour with little-known facts about Charleston. One house had pirate treasure buried in the backyard, according to legend; another was once lived in by the man who had brought the poinsettia to the United States; another was once lived in by the woman who was the inspiration for *Gone with the Wind*'s Melanie. She told him anything and everything she thought might make him see how special and how unique each house was.

Now it was late afternoon, and she was exhausted. She hadn't done this much walking or talking in years, she thought as she slipped off a shoe and surreptitiously rubbed her aching foot.

"We still have Fort Sumter and The Citadel to see,"

she said in a bright voice. She wasn't going to let Miles see how tired she was. "The Citadel is a school for—"

"I know what The Citadel is," Miles interrupted a little irritably. "We can see it another time. Right now it's hot, it's getting late, and I'm tired. I want something cold to drink and a nice leisurely dinner." He sat down beside her. "I expect you to have dinner with me," he added in a voice that brooked no disagreement. "After dragging me all around town today, it's the least you can do."

She bit back a sharp retort as she remembered her mission. Alienating him wouldn't do her any good. "Tomorrow—"

He interrupted her again. "Tomorrow we're getting out of town. This heat and humidity may not bother you, but I don't like it at all."

Claire turned her head and looked at him critically. He certainly didn't look as if the weather bothered him. He looked cool and crisp, and his shirt and pants were unwrinkled, as if he had just stepped out of the shower. She, on the other hand, felt like a limp dishrag and probably looked like one, too.

"It is unusually hot," she conceded. "It will take a thunderstorm to break this heat."

"If you're still determined to drag me around sightseeing tomorrow, we'll take a tour of the local beaches," he told her as he leaned back and draped an arm over the back of the bench.

"I do have a small beach house not too far from town," Claire said slowly. Suddenly a day at the beach sounded heavenly to her. She had never taken one of her guests to her beach house. She had always used it as a kind of private retreat. But Miles was different. "I suppose we could drive out there if you like," she said after a moment's consideration. After all, she thought, trying to justify her sudden invitation, she was taking him for a reason—a good reason.

Sarah would be proud of her for going to such lengths, she told herself, trying to ignore the little voice at the back of her mind that told her that she wanted to spend a day alone with Miles for reasons that had nothing to do with spying.

"I'd like that very much," he replied promptly. "Why don't we leave this afternoon? That way we can spend the whole day there tomorrow. We won't have to waste a lot of time driving."

"Leave now!" Claire exclaimed. The idea shocked her. "I couldn't do that."

"Why not?" he wanted to know. "Doesn't it have a bed?"

"Of course it has a bed." It was her turn to be irritated. "It has one bed," she said pointedly. "Where would you sleep?"

"With you," he answered immediately. He looked down and gave her a slightly wicked grin. "I'd enjoy that and so would you, once you got used to the idea."

Claire started to get up, but he put his hand on her arm and stopped her.

"Relax," he said. There was rich, warm laughter in his voice. "I'm only teasing. I love it when you get that shocked-southern-lady look on your face. If you only have one bed, what about the sofa? I could sleep there or on the floor."

Claire shook her head. "That's not a good idea," she said obstinately. "For one thing, the sofa is old and lumpy, and you wouldn't be comfortable on the floor, either."

"What you mean is, you wouldn't be comfortable," he said. He was suddenly watching her intently. "Why not? We're already sleeping under the same roof. What difference does it make where that roof is?"

This time Claire did get up. "It just does," she said lamely. She didn't even try to explain the difference.

How could she tell him her beach house was so small, she'd be aware of every breath he took? Here in Charleston, at least, they were separated by a long hall and a flight of stairs.

"Besides," she added suddenly, "I've got my other guests to think of. I can't leave town until they've had breakfast."

His eyes narrowed. "It's that damned house of yours," he growled.

Claire stiffened. She had no intention of listening to any criticism of her house.

"I never thought I'd be playing second fiddle to a piece of architecture," he grumbled. "If you'd hire someone to help you out, you'd be able to take some time off now and then."

"I don't want to take any time off. It was your idea to spend the night at the beach house," she pointed out reasonably, "not mine."

"You don't run that house of yours," he told her. The anger was dying out of his voice. "It runs you."

She turned and looked down at him. "I'm not complaining," she said quietly.

"No," he said with a resigned sigh. "That's just the trouble."

She started to move toward the street. "I'm going home," she threw over her shoulder. "Are you coming?"

He got to his feet and followed her. In a few strides he had caught up to her and taken her arm.

They had dinner in an old, restored tavern. Claire had suggested it because it was not a dark, intimate restaurant where people dined romantically. It was a cheerful, open kind of place that appealed to large groups of people rather than couples. Claire wasn't in the mood for romance, and she didn't want to give Miles any more ideas than he already had.

Still, by hook or by crook, and she wasn't quite sure how, he managed to secure the most secluded, the most intimate table in the place. Claire sat down reluctantly. She would have preferred a table that put them elbow to elbow with their neighbors. All through dinner, she prodded herself to ask him about the hotel he was planning to build. So far, she had to admit to herself, she wasn't being a very good spy.

Finally, over dessert, she took a deep breath. "Have you decided whether to put up a hotel here in Charleston?" she asked, trying to make it sound like a casual question.

He shook his head. "Not really," he answered. "I'm still looking around, trying to make up my mind."

Claire stared at the table so that he wouldn't see the expression in her eyes. More lies, she was thinking bitterly. For two cents she would have told him exactly what she thought of his duplicity.

"Where did you hear about my plans?" he asked. This time it was his voice that was deceptively casual.

"Oh, just around," she said vaguely. She gave him a sweet smile. "After all, you are Miles Sinclair, the owner of Hotels Americana. Someone was bound to recognize the name and put two and two together."

"I suppose so. Actually," he told her, "I'm not thinking of building from scratch. Buying and refurbishing an already existing hotel may be the way to go."

Claire's eyes grew cool. Miles was just digging himself in deeper and deeper as far as she was concerned. She *knew* he was planning on building just as soon as he acquired the property to build on.

"That sounds very expensive," she said. "It might be cheaper and easier to put up something new."

"I'm surprised to hear you say that," he commented. "As a die-hard preservationist, I'd think you'd fight me all the way."

"There are hotels, and there are hotels," she said, hoping he would think she wouldn't oppose him. He had to think she was on his side before he'd confide in her. A moment later, her words seemed justified.

"What would you think about a small inn? Something with about twenty-five rooms?"

"Twenty-five rooms!" she exclaimed. "That sounds fairly large to me."

"It's larger than what you've got, but smaller than a high-rise hotel," he pointed out.

"It would still require a good-size piece of property," she commented thoughtfully. "Do you have any property in mind?" she asked in what she hoped was a guileless tone.

"Oh, I have a few irons in the fire," he said easily. "But I'm still in the planning stage." He quickly changed the subject. "You still haven't told me what you think of my idea for an inn."

Claire stared at the table. She knew she should rave over all his ideas so that he would confide in her, but she couldn't, she just couldn't. "I don't like it," she said finally. "I can see that it might work in some places, but not here."

"Why not?"

"For one thing, there are a lot of problems you haven't taken into consideration. What about parking? That's a problem now. Where are the guests going to park? For that matter, where are your employees going to park? And what about deliveries? A small bed and breakfast with four rooms is one thing; the kind of thing you're proposing is another."

Her objections didn't seem to bother him in the least.

"I didn't think you'd like it," he said calmly. "But I think you'd like a big hotel even less. Look, Claire, I'm not an ogre."

"I never said you were!" she exclaimed at once.

"No, but you're thinking it. I didn't come to Charleston to destroy anything."

Claire stared at him thoughtfully. Was this the truth? She doubted it. Sincere though he sounded, he was very good at avoiding her questions. Instinct told her . . . She shook her head impatiently and dismissed the thought. She was beginning to think she couldn't trust her own instincts where Miles was concerned. Like it or not, her feelings for him, confused though they were, kept clouding her judgment.

He signaled for the waiter. "Let's get out of here. I enjoyed our meal," he added as they walked through the hot, humid evening toward her house. "But it wasn't the kind of restaurant I would have picked out for us." He gave her a sideward glance. "I suspect you know that already."

Claire merely smiled. "I'll say good night," she said

when they reached her house. "It's late, and we've got a busy day ahead of us tomorrow."

"It's not that late," Miles told her. "I'm going to have some of that brandy I bought. Would you like some?"

"No, thanks."

"Then you can keep me company while I drink some," he said persuasively. He gave her an irresistible smile. "Please."

"Just for a few minutes," Claire said uneasily. "Then I've got to get to bed."

Miles grinned. It was a lazy, seductive smile. "You could go to bed right now if you'd take me with you," he said to her wickedly.

"I'm not going to stay down here if you talk like that," Claire replied coldly. She walked into the drawing room and poured some brandy into one of the glasses she had left out just for him. She handed it to him, then began switching on lamps, flooding the room with light.

Miles followed her around, turning off the lights.

"What are you doing?" she demanded, outraged.

"We don't need the lights on. There's a big, full moon out there," he replied. "These tall windows of yours let in plenty of light." He put his glass on the table and his voice changed abruptly. "I wish for once," he told her with sudden anger, "just for once, that you'd stop running from me."

"I'm not running from you," she said indignantly. How many times did she have to say it?

"Oh yes, you are," he said with savagery that surprised her. "Every time I get near you, you jump."

Claire bit back a sharp retort. Arguing with him wouldn't do her any good. "Well, you do make me a little

93

nervous," she said in her best southern belle voice. She stopped herself just before she batted her eyelids at him.

"Come and sit down," he said a little more gently.

Claire felt her feet taking her toward him. She sat down on the sofa next to him, being careful to keep her body stiff and erect. Miles, on the other hand, leaned back and made himself comfortable.

"Claire," he asked after a few moments. "Why do I make you so nervous?" He sat up, put his hands on her shoulders, and turned her so that she had to face him. "Look at me," he urged her. "Look into my eyes. Why are you so afraid to trust me?"

Claire looked into his eyes. In the moonlight, she could see the urgency there. His eyes were so compelling that she began to feel a little of that urgency herself.

"You haven't exactly given me much reason to trust you," she said uncertainly.

"I've given you every reason to trust me," he responded in a voice that had grown even more gentle. "And you know it. That's why you're sitting here now. But for some reason, you can't admit it. I want to know why."

She tried to look away, but she couldn't. "I'm afraid of being hurt," she whispered against her will.

"I'm not going to hurt you," he replied. His dark, compelling eyes were still intent on hers. Her body began to tingle. She immediately lowered her own eyes so he wouldn't see what she was feeling.

"You're only here for a couple of weeks," she reminded him. "After that you'll be leaving me with a casual goodbye and a few bittersweet memories. That's what I'm afraid of."

He captured her chin with his hand and held it firmly.

Claire risked another look into his face and almost drowned in the warmth she saw there. Why was it Miles who made her feel like this? she asked herself a little frantically.

"I don't have to leave," he told her. "I'll stay forever if that's what you want."

Claire suddenly wanted to believe him, but instinct told her she didn't dare. He'd lied over and over about his hotel; he was probably lying about this, too. "You say that now," she told him, still striving to keep her voice even, "but what will you say after . . ." She couldn't say the words. She bit her lower lip.

He said them for her. "After we've made love?" he asked softly.

She nodded unhappily, pulled away from him and got to her feet. She couldn't sit next to him any longer. She walked over to one of the tall, graceful windows and stared out at the moon-drenched garden. Miles immediately followed her.

"I'll say exactly the same thing," he told her softly. He leaned toward her, but Claire stopped him.

"Don't kiss me," she said. In the rich moonlight, her eyes pleaded with him to understand. "Not now. I need some time to think. Everything is moving too quickly."

He lightly touched his lips to her forehead. "All right. I won't press you anymore tonight. Sweet dreams," he said in a voice that gave Claire the idea he had to force himself to leave her.

"Good night," she said a little forlornly.

Some spy she was, she thought as she stood alone in the moonlight. All she had learned tonight was that she was more and more attracted to a man who lied to her.

CHAPTER SIX

"Maybe we should go to the beach another day," Claire
said as she cast a nervous glance through the window and
up at the sky. The morning was sullen, humid, and heavily overcast. "Rain is predicted, and it could be quite
heavy." Breakfast was over, and she was reluctantly
packing some food in a picnic basket. He had come into
the kitchen to hurry her up.

"A little rain won't hurt us," Miles told her.

"A little rain isn't what I'm worried about," she replied tartly. "The weather report—"

"I heard the weather report this morning myself," he
interrupted, "and it's nothing to worry about. Let's go
and enjoy ourselves. If the weather turns bad, we can
always leave."

"All right," Claire said. She was as anxious as Miles to
get away for the day; she just didn't want to admit it—
not to him, anyway. She had always loved the beach; it
was a wonderful place for her to rest and recharge her
batteries.

"What are these barrier islands?" Miles asked as they
drove out of town.

"They're small islands just off the coast that protect
the mainland," she told him. "Charlestonians have had

summer homes on them since before the war. My house is a very small place, and it's certainly not fancy," she cautioned. "I hope you aren't expecting much."

His eyes left the road for a moment and touched her face. "As long as I'm with you, I don't care where we are," he said.

Claire stared out the window at the flat, marshy land without really seeing it. Those were nice-sounding words, she was thinking. He sounded so sincere. But he always sounded sincere, she reminded herself. She was beginning to have a hard time telling what was real about him and what was a lie.

A few moments later, they were pulling up to her gray, weathered cottage. As she had told him, it wasn't very large, and it stood on stilts to protect it from incoming high tides. It was surrounded by sand and palmettos.

"This is it," she said. She looked at the cottage with pleasure. She loved it almost as much as she loved her graceful old double house.

"It needs a coat of paint," Miles observed as she led him up the steep, weather-beaten steps to the door.

"It needs a lot of things," Claire replied. She opened the door and stepped inside. "Unfortunately, the Charleston house comes first."

He gave her a wry look. "It always seems to come first." He put his strong hands on her arms. "Let's not have any talk about houses or hotels," he suggested.

Claire looked up at him. The look in his eyes was so warm that she had to stop herself from stepping forward into his arms. For a moment his touch threw her off balance. Then she gave herself a mental shake.

"That sounds like a good idea to me," she said, though she had no intention of doing that. She had brought him here for the express purpose of talking about houses and hotels.

"For the rest of the day, we'll just be a man and a woman enjoying the beach and each other," he murmured in his arresting voice. "Nothing will exist but the two of us." His hands tightened on her arms. Claire forgot about being a spy and took a step toward him.

He kissed her then, and Claire didn't even try to pull away. When their lips met, she realized she didn't want to leave his arms. Miles was right about one thing, she thought just before her mind stopped working entirely. There *was* some kind of magic whenever their lips touched. She didn't understand it, she didn't even like it, but it existed. And no matter how much she tried, she couldn't seem to get away from it. Miles wouldn't let her.

A moment later, the intensity of the kiss began to frighten her. She felt a pulsating passion that, after only one kiss, was threatening to escalate.

Abruptly, she pushed him away and raised a shaky hand to her lips. "What do you think you proved by that?" she asked a little unsteadily.

"That you want me as much as I want you," he answered at once. His voice was tight and desire-roughened. He jammed his hands into his pockets and watched her through narrowed eyes.

Claire turned away and went over to the windows overlooking the ocean.

"Sooner or later you're going to have to face facts and—" he began.

Claire swung around and glared at him. "No," she cried out. "Sooner or later *you're* going to have to face the fact that you can't get what you want by seducing me." As soon as the words were out, she knew she had made a mistake.

"I don't know what you're talking about," he said flatly. "I don't want to seduce you. I want to make love to you."

Claire stared at him, and he stared back.

"Let's go for a swim," she said finally. Anything, she was thinking, anything to defuse this situation. "You can change in the bathroom," she added.

To her surprise, Miles chuckled. It was an infectious sound. "Naturally. I wouldn't want to offend your sensibilities," he teased her.

While he was changing, Claire quickly unpacked the picnic basket, then went into the bedroom to change into her own bathing suit. It was a simple black maillot, almost conservative in style, that she had worn for years. Once she had it on, she surveyed herself in the small mirror over the dressing table. For a moment, she wished she were wearing something with a little more pizazz. Then a faint smile turned her lips up slightly. It really didn't matter what she was wearing. Miles seemed to find her attractive in whatever she put on. She pulled a bright pink shirt over it, tied the ends around her waist, and hurried back into the living room.

Miles whistled when he saw her. "Nice legs," he commented approvingly as his eyes flicked over her in a way that was anything but casual. "Nice everything else, too," he added when his eyes returned to her face.

"You're not so bad looking yourself," Claire said lightly, trying her best Mata Hari voice. He wore a pair of thin nylon trunks, the kind used by swimmers to cut down on water resistance. His dark, hairy chest was uncovered, and Claire's fingers started to itch as she wondered what it would feel like to run them across it.

As she realized what she was thinking, she turned away and busied herself with the beach towels, hoping he didn't notice her interest.

"Come on," he said suddenly. "I'll race you down to the beach." The door overlooking the beach banged shut behind him.

Claire grabbed the towels and ran after him. She hurried across the porch that stretched along the front of her house, down the stairs that led to the beach, and over the dunes that mounded protectively in front of her cottage. But it was too late. Miles had too big a head start on her. She came to a breathless stop beside him and dropped the towels onto the sand.

"You won." She laughed up at him. She pushed her hair from her face. After a sprint across the beach, it was a glorious tumble.

"Yes, but what did I win?" he asked meaningfully. His eyes dropped to her soft mouth.

Claire missed his provocative glance. She was too busy looking around her.

"There aren't many people on the beach," she said a little worriedly. There were one or two people on the sand, and practically no one was in the water. "On a day like this the beach is usually packed with people. Maybe we should have listened to the weather report again before we came down."

Now that she got a good look at it, she saw that the ocean wasn't its usual blue-green color. It was as gray as the clouds. It was rough, too, not gentle, as it pounded the beach.

"We can listen when we go in for lunch," Miles said

imperturbably. "I came down here to swim, and I'm going to swim."

"I don't know," Claire said. There was doubt in her voice. "It looks awfully rough out there."

"Those waves?" he scoffed. "Have you ever seen the waves in California? These are nothing compared to those. Look at those people in the water. They aren't having any trouble."

He took her by the hand and led her toward the water. Claire didn't offer much resistance. She liked the feel of her hand in his.

He looked around suddenly and seemed to read her thoughts.

"It seems to belong, doesn't it?" he asked softly. He smiled down at her with a smile so warm, it made Claire's heart miss a beat.

"What belongs where?" she asked a little incoherently.

"Your hand in mine," he answered simply. He lifted it to his lips and kissed the back of her hand. All the while, his eyes were watching her.

At the touch of his lips, Claire felt a small, earthquake-type tremor rock her world, and for a moment, just for a moment, she wished she were in his arms. She jerked her hand away and walked past him. She didn't stop until the water was lapping at her ankles. Behind her, she could hear Miles chuckling softly.

"We came here to swim," she reminded him.

"So we did," he answered. He took hold of her hand again and began pulling her into the water. "Once we get past that first row of breakers, we'll be all right."

Claire let him pull her deeper and deeper into the water. With his hand firmly clasping hers, she felt perfectly safe, even when the waves buffeted her as they came crashing toward the shore. It wasn't until he let go of her hand that she began to feel a little alarmed. There was a strong undertow that the ocean didn't usually have. It seemed to pull her away from the beach even when she was swimming toward it. Treading water as best she could, she turned to look for Miles. With long powerful strokes, he was swimming away from her. The undertow didn't seem to bother him.

Then suddenly he disappeared.

"Miles!" she called out. She looked around frantically, but there was no one who could help. All at once, she realized they were the only people in the water. A raindrop from above hit her on the face. It was beginning to sprinkle, and the few people on the beach were starting to leave.

"Miles!" she called again. This time the panic in her voice was evident. She didn't know what to do.

Then, much to her relief, he surfaced beside her. Claire grabbed him and held on tight. She wasn't going to let him go again.

Miles's hands encircled her waist. "Well, well," he said in her ear, "I didn't expect a greeting like this." Then he looked down at her face. "What's wrong?" he asked at once. His hands tightened around her waist.

"You disappeared," she said with a gulp. "I looked around, and I couldn't find you."

"Well, here I am," he said soothingly. "There's nothing to worry about. It takes more than a few waves to get rid of me. You ought to know that by now."

"I think we ought to go in," Claire told him uneasily. "It's raining."

"It's just sprinkling a little," he corrected her. His hands began to move up and down her back. "Besides, I don't want to go in yet. I'm just starting to enjoy this," he said wickedly. "It isn't every day you cling to me with such abandon."

"I'm not clinging to you," Claire protested at once, though that was exactly what she was doing. The motion of the water was growing stronger and stronger, and she wasn't sure she had the strength to withstand it.

"There's nothing to worry about," Miles said. "I can touch the bottom here."

"I can't," Claire retorted a little irritably. "And I'm getting worried. I've never seen the ocean quite like this."

"Wrap your legs around my waist," he instructed her. "It'll make you feel safer." His voice was smooth, but there was a sudden glint in his eye. He was obviously enjoying this situation.

"I doubt it," Claire said shortly.

A moment later, however, a wave threatened to separate them, and she did just what he had suggested.

"Miles," she said, trying to keep the fear out of her voice, "it's really raining now. Let's go in." It seemed to her as if the waves were crashing all around them. Any minute now, she expected one to crash over them.

"We're already wet," he told her reasonably. "What difference does a little rain make?" He looked down and saw her face. It was white, and her blue eyes were dark with fear. "All right," he said gently. "I won't tease you anymore. We'll go in."

Claire breathed a sigh of relief. She was so frightened. She was ready to let go of Miles and swim for shore by herself, but she knew she'd feel safer with him beside her.

"I'm going to let go of you," Miles told her encouragingly, "and just hold your hand. But don't worry. I won't let anything happen to you."

"I know," Claire said a little shakily. "It's just that the waves are so big, and the shore looks so far away."

"I know," he said with surprising understanding, "but it isn't really far at all. Now, don't worry," he told her again. "I've been in the ocean when it's been a whole lot rougher than this. There's nothing to be afraid of."

Claire nodded. Her teeth were beginning to chatter. "Let's go," she said.

"You'll have to let go of me first," Miles said. There was laughter in his voice, but it didn't annoy her. For once, she was grateful for his self-confidence.

She grimaced and forced herself to let go of him. A moment later they were swimming toward the beach. Claire was just beginning to think they would make it when a wave broke over them. It pushed her down to the ocean floor and would have pulled her backward if it hadn't been for Miles. He held on to her and kept her from being sucked out to deeper water.

Finally, after what seemed like an endless amount of time to Claire, they were standing in knee-deep water and the breakers were behind them.

"I wasn't sure we were going to make it," she told him in what she hoped was a light tone of voice. Now that they were safe, she was a little embarrassed by how frightened she'd been.

"Getting back in was rougher than I expected," Miles conceded. "Those waves are a lot stronger than they seem." He looked down at her. There was concern in his eyes. "I hope I didn't hurt you," he said. "There were a couple of minutes when I was afraid to let go of you."

Claire looked down at her arm. She could see vivid red marks where his fingers had been gripping her. "You didn't hurt me," she assured him. "I didn't even notice.

I'm just glad you didn't let go." She glanced up at the sky. It was growing darker by the minute. "I think we're in for a real downpour," she said as she began wading out of the knee-deep water.

At that moment a wave rushed in from behind them and pushed her forward. At the same time, the undertow caught her around the ankles. She would have been knocked over if it hadn't been for Miles. He saw her stagger and caught her in his arms before she could fall.

They had nearly reached the steps leading to her house when the heavens opened up. Claire slid her arms around Miles's neck and clung to him when he picked her up and took the stairs two at a time. By the time they reached the shelter of the porch, she was laughing. Her fear had left her; now she was simply glad to be alive, glad to be with Miles. He lowered her to her feet, then looked down at her.

"What's so funny?" he wanted to know.

"Nothing, really," she said between giggles. "It's just the way you sprinted up the steps so we wouldn't get wet —after we'd nearly drowned in the ocean."

He grinned back at her. "I guess it was a little silly," he admitted. "But I was worried. I could feel you trembling as I held you." He put his hands out and grasped her by her arms. "You're not trembling now," he said softly.

"No," she said breathlessly. She wasn't trembling outwardly, at least. But inside, something was fluttering wildly in her stomach. With great difficulty she detached herself from his grasp. "I think we'd better change into something dry," she said. "It's getting cold."

"You're right," Miles said. "You've got goose bumps." He looked around him in surprise. In between the time they had left the cottage for their swim and the time they had returned, the temperature must have dropped twenty-five degrees.

Claire nodded. Unfortunately, she thought to herself, her goose bumps weren't caused by the cold.

"Go take a warm shower," Miles told her, "while I build a fire." He looked down at her and grinned mischievously. "Unless, of course, you want me to scrub your back."

"I can manage by myself, thank you," Claire said with a hint of asperity.

"Are you sure?" Miles asked. He reached out and turned her so that she was looking directly at him. The mischievousness of his smile turned a little wicked. At the look in his eyes, Claire had to will herself not to blush. "You may not realize it, but I'm very good with my hands."

"Then I suggest you use them to build the fire," she said a little breathlessly.

He reached for her and drew her against his long, hard body. Claire put her hands up as a barrier and found them resting on his still-damp chest. She was surprised at how warm it was and how coarse the curling tendrils of hair felt beneath her fingers.

"That's exactly what I'd like to do," he said sensually. "I'd like to build a fire in you that only I can put out." He lowered his head. "What do you say, Claire?" he whispered urgently against her lips. "We're alone here. No one will disturb us. Let me love you."

She opened her mouth to reply, and Miles seized the opportunity to take possession of her. She felt his tongue move between her trembling lips, and as it did so, something turned over deep inside her. Her fingers tightened on his chest, and she could feel the rapid beating of his

106

heart beneath her palm. It gave her a heady feeling to know that she was the reason for its pounding.

"Claire," he murmured hoarsely, "I want you so much. Every time I see you, I want you even more." His hands slid masterfully up and down her bare back. It wasn't long before Claire's entire body was trembling, not with cold or fright, but with desire.

Without thinking, she wrapped her arms around his neck and let her head fall back to welcome his kisses.

His hands slid farther down her back until he was cupping her buttocks in his hands. Claire felt a mindless thrill of excitement as he pressed her hips to his. Then, as the intimacy of the gesture threatened to increase, excitement gave way to an attack of nerves. If she gave in to him now, knowing how he'd lied to her, she'd probably regret it for the rest of her life. She tried to pull away, but it wasn't easy.

While her mind was telling her she had to put a stop to his lovemaking, her body was pressing itself against him and clamoring for more. When his hips began to gyrate slowly against hers and she heard herself moan softly in response, she knew she had only a few seconds to act before passion replaced reason entirely.

She forced herself to pull her reluctant lips from his, forced herself to step out of his arms. Hardest of all was forcing herself to look up at him, at the marked desire on his face, but she did that, too.

"What is it?" he demanded harshly. "What's the matter?" He reached for her impatiently.

Claire took two steps backward and averted her eyes. The hunger in his face upset her. She wondered if she had the same unfulfilled look on her face.

"I asked you not to rush me," she said quietly.

"Rush you!" he burst out. "I've never been so patient in all my life!"

"Then be patient a little longer," Claire begged. "I'm —I'm confused," she confessed. That, she thought ruefully, was an understatement. She was attracted to a man, she was actually considering making love to a man, who did nothing but lie to her.

"All right," he said with a sigh. "I don't understand why you're so confused, but I'll wait. I have a feeling you're going to be worth waiting for."

"I wish you wouldn't talk like that," she said uncomfortably.

"I know you do. But you're going to have to realize that there's something very special between us."

There are nothing but lies between us, she silently responded.

"What happens between us is far more than physical," he went on. "Lovemaking is not sex. I don't want or need you for sex. I can find that anywhere."

Claire turned away so he wouldn't see her blush and walked over to the window. The rain was coming down in sheets now, but she didn't notice.

"Turn around," Miles commanded in a voice that was used to being obeyed. "Turn around and look at me."

Instinctively, Claire did as she was told. He got up and crossed the room. When he reached her, he put his hands on her arms and forced her to look up at him. Immediately, the magnetism began to flow between them.

He spoke in a voice so arresting it was almost hypnotic. "If you knew more about it, you'd realize that lovemaking involves more than the body. It also involves the heart and the mind."

I don't want my heart or my mind involved, Claire

thought. I don't want to be involved with someone I can't trust. She shook her head wearily and pulled away from him.

Miles studied her face for a moment before he spoke. "Why don't you go take your shower?" he said finally. "I'll see about that fire. Have you got any wood?"

"It's in the woodbox," Claire answered as she made her escape from the room. "And there are matches in the kitchen." She was glad to be getting away from Miles. Being with him was like being on an emotional roller coaster. One minute she was up, the next minute she was down, and frequently she didn't have any idea at all where she was.

She took a hurried shower, then put on a pair of faded jeans and a sweater. After we eat lunch, we're leaving, she vowed to herself. Bringing him to the beach hadn't been a good idea at all. It was one thing to be alone with him in her double house; it was another to be alone with him here.

"It's all yours," she said, gesturing toward the bathroom.

Miles was warming himself in front of the fire. He sat back on his heels and looked at her. "I've never seen you in jeans before," he commented appreciatively.

"I don't wear them in town," she said a little self-consciously. The look on his face was making her uncomfortable.

"You ought to," he said. "You've certainly got the figure for them."

"Why don't you take a shower while I get lunch ready?" she said. She was glad to change the subject. "Then I think we should be leaving. The rain is really coming down now."

Claire busied herself in the kitchen until he disappeared. She was afraid to have him come close to her. She was afraid of what might happen if he touched her again, or if she touched him.

"I don't think we should wait to eat lunch," Claire said when Miles emerged from his shower. "It's getting worse out there. We'd better leave right away."

"But I'm hungry," Miles protested.

"We can eat in the car," she told him. "Just listen to that wind! If we don't leave now, we may not be able to."

Miles grinned. "Would that be so bad?" he asked. There was a glint in his eyes that Claire didn't like.

"You know it would be," she snapped. She didn't know which was making her more nervous—the weather or Miles's closeness. With hands that weren't quite steady, she began dumping food back into the picnic basket.

"We can't leave now," he told her reasonably. "It's raining so hard, the windshield wipers won't work." From the other side of the counter he began unpacking the food she was stowing away. "It'll ease up in a while. It can't rain like this for long. It's nothing more than a passing storm." He began stacking the sandwiches she had made onto a plate. "It won't take us long to eat, and while we're eating we can get a weather report on the radio."

While Miles ate and Claire picked at her food, the rain grew heavier and the wind stronger. Miles seemed oblivious to what was going on outside, but Claire stared at the window grimly. This was no passing storm, and she knew it.

Finally, they heard the weather on the radio. Tropical storm Bob had changed direction and was now heading straight toward the coast. Though the winds of the storm hadn't reached hurricane speed, the storm was intensifying, and everyone was advised to stay off the roads except for a case of extreme emergency.

"Stay tuned to this station for further details," the announcer told them at the end of the report.

Claire stared at the radio in horror for a long moment as the meaning of the weather report sank in. Then the uncertain flickering of the lights brought her to her feet.

"We've got to go right now," she said urgently. "We should never have stayed long enough to eat."

Miles poured himself another cup of coffee and leaned back in his chair. "Didn't you hear the man?" he asked, gesturing toward the radio. "We're supposed to stay off the roads."

Claire gaped at him. "We can't stay here!" she cried. "I've got to get back to Charleston! I've got guests to take care of! Besides . . ." her voice dwindled away.

"It's that *besides* that's really bothering you, isn't it?" he asked shrewdly. "You're afraid we'll have to spend the night here, and you don't like it."

"You planned this," Claire accused him suddenly. "You knew this would happen if we stayed long enough to have lunch!"

Miles grinned at that. "You're giving me a little too much credit," he said mildly. "Even I can't arrange a tropical storm when I want one."

He cradled the coffee cup in his hands and looked at her over the top of it. There was amusement and something Claire couldn't quite identify in his eyes. Whatever it was, she didn't like it.

"I have to admit, though," he added smoothly, "that I don't mind what Mother Nature has thrown our way. I'm going to enjoy spending the night here with you. It's a lot more cozy and intimate here than at your house in town."

"We are not staying here!" Claire all but shouted. "We're leaving right now."

"Claire, we're not going anywhere." Miles put his coffee cup back on its saucer and stood up. He was suddenly as angry as she was. "I'm not going to risk my life driving in weather like this just because you're afraid to be alone with me."

Claire glared at him. "If you won't go with me, I'll just have to go by myself," she told him coldly.

"That won't be easy," he said. Something jingled in his hand, and he held it up for her to see. It was a key ring. "I have the car keys, and I'm not about to give them to you. Of course," he added wickedly, "you can always try and take them from me. That would be an interesting way to spend the afternoon."

Claire ignored that. She started for the door leading to the porch.

"Since you won't take me back to Charleston," she told him evenly, "I'll find someone who will."

"Don't be ridiculous, Claire," Miles said. His annoyance was obvious. "You can't go out there. It's—"

The rest of his words were lost as Claire yanked open the door. She staggered onto the porch and tried to look around her. But the rain was coming down so hard that visibility was practically nonexistent. She could see some lights shining dimly from the other houses, but she knew she'd never be able to fight the wind long enough to get to one of them. Even on her porch it was an effort just to keep from being blown this way and that. Whether she liked it or not, she was alone with Miles, as alone as if they were marooned on a desert island. Defeated, she went back inside. Miles was waiting for her with a towel.

"See what I mean?" he asked as he began patting her with it.

Claire snatched the towel from his hands. "I can do that for myself," she snapped.

"I don't mind doing it for you," he replied. "In fact, I like doing it."

Claire walked around him and headed for the telephone. She picked it up and breathed a sigh of relief. It was still working. Quickly, she dialed Sarah's number.

"Where are you?" Sarah wanted to know. "Isn't this weather terrible?"

"We're still at the beach," Claire told her friend grimly. "We can't get back."

"That's wonderful!" Sarah cried. She didn't seem to notice the tension in Claire's voice. "You'll have to spend the night there. This is the perfect time for you to work on Miles and to get him to tell you his plans."

Claire looked over at Miles and saw that he was watching her. She hoped he couldn't hear what Sarah had said. She turned her back on him and spoke into the phone.

"I've got guests at my house," she said. "I know it's a lot to ask, but could you spend the night there and see that they get some kind of breakfast?"

Sarah groaned. "I don't even cook for myself—" she began.

"There are several different kinds of bread in the freezer," Claire interrupted quickly. "All you have to do is slice the loaves and serve some fruit. I'll be back as soon as I can."

"All right," Sarah said with a sigh that was audible over the phone.

113

"Thanks, Sarah," Claire said gratefully. "I really appreciate it."

"It's all right," Sarah told her. "But you'd better come home with some good information to make all this worthwhile. If I'd known—"

The phone went dead. Claire put it down. Now she and Miles were even more alone than before. She turned to face him with a feeling akin to panic.

"What is it?" he asked quizzically.

"The phone lines are down," she told him. "I suppose it's only a matter of time—"

Outside there was a flash of brilliant white lightning, followed by a crash of thunder. Almost simultaneously, the lights flickered, then went out.

"—before we lose the electricity," she finished shakily. She cast a nervous look at the window.

"Well," Miles said philosophically, "we've still got the fire, and there's plenty of dry wood in the woodbox. Do you have a flashlight?"

"No," she answered. "But there are some oil lamps in the cupboard."

A few moments later, the lamps were bathing the living room in a mellow glow. In spite of the storm outside, the warmth of the fire and the light of the lamps made the room seem warm and inviting. Miles seemed to think so, too.

"We may as well make the best of this," he told her. He had been rooting around in the cupboard. "There are some cans of food in here—"

"The stove is electric," Claire told him dampeningly. She wasn't in the mood to make the best of things.

"—some sterno to heat it with, an old chess game, and this." With great care he held up an old dusty bottle. "I found this in the back of the cupboard. It must have been there for years." There was such awe in his voice that Claire went to see what he was holding.

"What is it?" she asked.

"This," he told her as he carried it over to the counter, "is a bottle of very old French burgundy. It ought to be wonderful, but it hasn't exactly been stored in ideal conditions. I wonder who left it there."

"It must have been my grandfather," Claire said. She perched on a barstool and watched him. "You're not going to open it, are you?"

"Of course I am," he answered. "What could be more perfect to drink on an afternoon like this than a glass of red wine? While we're drinking it, we can play chess."

"Chess?" Claire asked faintly.

"Why not? We've got to do something, and you don't seem interested in the other activities I could suggest."

"Chess is fine," she said quickly. She began setting up the game on the small round table where they had eaten lunch.

"Not there," Miles said as he slowly and expertly uncorked the wine. "In front of the fireplace."

Claire glanced at him suspiciously, but he seemed to be concentrating on the wine. She picked up the game and carried it over to the rug in front of the fireplace. He was right, she thought with a sigh. It was warmer there, and the fire gave off a comforting light.

"I had no idea it could be this cold in June," she commented when he dropped down onto the floor across from her.

He handed her a jelly glass half full of wine. "I couldn't find any wineglasses," he told her. "I hope it doesn't bother you to drink out of these." Before she

115

could answer, he leaned over and clinked his glass against hers. "To us," he said softly. "To our first night alone. May we have many more."

Claire started to object, but the look on his face stopped her. Why waste time arguing over something as meaningless as a toast? she asked herself. Instead, she raised the wine to her lips and tasted it. It was unlike any other wine she had ever tasted. She watched Miles as he rolled it around his mouth.

"Liquid rubies," he said finally. "I can think of only one thing that tastes better." His eyes dropped suggestively to her mouth. "Claire . . ." he began in a voice that wasn't quite his own.

She picked up a pawn. "Shall I move first, or do you want to?" she asked brightly.

Two and a half hours later, the wine was half gone and she had beaten Miles four times.

"You let me win," Claire accused him.

He shook his head. "I never let anyone win. Let's just say my mind was on other things," he said meaningfully. She looked up and met his glance. The look in his eye made her stomach turn a sommersault.

"Other things?" she echoed confusedly. She wished he didn't make her feel this way.

"You," he told her in a deep, lazy voice.

Claire focused on the chessboard. She felt safer looking at it than into his eyes. "Why don't we turn the radio back on?" she suggested uncomfortably as she began putting the pieces of the game away. "Maybe the storm is moving on and we'll be able to leave soon."

Before the words were quite out of her mouth, there was a brilliant flash of lightning, followed by a burst of thunder. Claire winced. Outside, lightning began to light

116

up the sky. She got to her feet, went over to the windows, and yanked the curtains closed.

When she returned to her spot in front of the fireplace and finished putting away the chessmen, her hands were shaking. Overhead, there was another crash of thunder. It was so loud this time that the cottage seemed to shake.

"Does thunder bother you?" Miles asked. He took the chess pieces from her fingers and put them in the box.

"A little," she confessed. "When I was a child, it used to terrify me. I used to hide in bed with the covers pulled over my head until it was over."

"By yourself?" Miles asked. He sounded a little shocked. "Didn't anyone console you?"

She shook her head. "My mother was dead, and my father believes in facing your fears."

"You don't have to be alone now," Miles told her. He gathered her into his arms, and they sat staring at the fire until the thunder and lightning passed.

"I'm afraid we're going to be here all night," he said finally.

That was exactly what Claire feared. The prospect made her almost as nervous as the thunder had. Considering the way she responded to that magnetism of his, she knew she had good cause to be nervous.

"I may as well get dinner ready," he said. "It's after six."

"You?" she asked in surprise.

"Of course me," he said. "Why not?"

"I didn't know you could cook."

"There are lots of things you don't know about me. I happen to be a very good cook."

"Then you're in charge," she said promptly. "I'm good at breakfasts, and that's about it. I'll set the table."

She set the table, all the while wishing night weren't approaching quite so quickly. She knew, she just knew, that Miles was going to be difficult. She was sure he was going to object to sleeping on the sofa by himself—and not for reasons of comfort, either.

Once the table was set, she sat down and watched him. He opened several cans, mixed them together, and added some of this and some of that from the cupboard. When he put her plate in front of her, Claire looked at it dubiously.

He saw her eyeing it. "Try to think of it as beef burgundy," he suggested. "Would you like more wine?"

"Yes, please," she said. She hoped it would give her a little courage.

He poured more wine into her jelly glass, sat down across from her, and watched expectantly as she tasted her food.

"It's delicious," she said. She was astonished. "I can't believe this came out of a can."

"Several cans, actually," he said complacently as he began to eat. "When we get back to Charleston, I'll prepare a real dinner for you."

He ate heartily while Claire toyed nervously with her food, trying to make the meal last as long as possible. After they ate, they washed the dishes and cleaned up the kitchen. In fact, Claire cleaned it so well that it almost sparkled. She scrubbed the counters and washed the cabinets. She did everything but clean the oven, and she would have done that, too, if she'd had anything to clean it with. Finally, there was nothing left to do.

Miles took the sponge from her hands, tossed it into the sink, and looked down at her. In the light from the oil lamps, she could see his eyes glittering dangerously. She gulped.

"We're finished," he said with that smooth confidence that never failed to annoy her. "There's nothing to do now but go to bed."

CHAPTER SEVEN

There was a long, tense silence after Miles's words, then Claire pulled herself together. She wasn't going to let him provoke her. Now was the time to let him know she had no intention of sleeping with him.

"Fine," she said coolly. "I'll sleep in the bedroom and you can take the sofa."

"That's not what I had in mind," he told her.

"I'm sure it isn't," she answered dryly.

"You'll be cold in there," he said. "You'd better sleep out here with me. I'll see that you stay warm."

Claire didn't doubt that. Just the thought of sleeping with him made her feel warm all over.

"I won't be cold," she told him in what she hoped was a quelling tone. "I've got plenty of blankets."

"Then how about another glass of wine before we say good night?" Miles suggested. Clearly he didn't want their evening to end. "There's a little left, and it would be a shame to waste it."

"No thanks," Claire said briefly.

"Oh, come on," Miles urged her. "Stop thinking of me as the big bad wolf. Another glass of wine won't do any harm." He looked at her in such an appealing fashion that Claire relented.

"It's been over an hour since we heard a weather report," he said with a smile. "We may as well find out what's going on out there." He turned on the radio.

"All we have to do is listen to the wind and the rain to know what's going on," Claire said as she curled up in a big overstuffed chair and sipped her wine. "I'm beginning to think this storm will never end."

"Oh, it will end," Miles told her regretfully. He sat down on the sofa and looked over at her. "Most good things do, eventually."

Claire stared into her glass and didn't say a word. They sat in silence through the news and the weather report. She told herself she felt only relief when the forecaster announced that the storm would start moving up the coast by morning.

"We should be back in town in time for breakfast," she said with brightness she didn't feel. Suddenly, she didn't want to leave the cottage. Now that she knew their time alone together would be ending soon, she found she was enjoying it. She finished her wine and put the glass down.

At that moment, the sounds of Glenn Miller filled the small cottage, and the radio announcer welcomed them to the Glenn Miller hour.

Miles walked over to her and lifted her out of her chair. Claire was too surprised to resist.

"Let's dance," he said as he pulled her into his arms.

"Dance?" she echoed uncertainly. His arms had encircled her, making it hard for her to breathe.

As they began dancing, her uneasiness was replaced by a sense of exhilaration. Outside, the wind was howling and the rain was beating down on her cottage, but inside she felt safe and warm. Something in the way Miles was holding her was making her feel cherished. She relaxed

121

and let herself enjoy the feeling. She was beginning to believe she *did* belong in his arms, just as he claimed. In spite of his lies, in spite of her doubts about him, she liked having him hold her. She relaxed a little more, and their dancing slowed perceptibly. Before long, they were doing nothing more than swaying in each other's arms.

"We seem to do our dancing in some pretty strange places," Miles said eventually. His voice was husky and slightly breathless. "First, the summer house at Ashley Plantation, then during a near-hurricane. At least this time we have music."

"We had music last time, too," Claire pointed out.

"If you call the chirping of crickets and the croaking of frogs music," Miles replied. There was an undercurrent of rich, masculine laughter to his voice.

She peeked up at him. "I do call those things music," she said shyly. "I hate to admit it, but that was one of the most romantic evenings of my life."

"I'm glad," he said simply. "And I'm glad you told me." He gazed down at her. "I'm going to do everything I can to make sure this night is even more memorable."

Claire shivered in his arms, but she didn't say anything. Her mouth was suddenly dry and she was too nervous to speak.

She felt a thrill of jittery expectation run down her back as Miles's arms tightened around her waist. His long fingers spread out along her spine and seemed to cover all of her back and hips. He lifted one hand up and ran it through her dark hair. Gently he tugged her head back until she was looking up at him. Their eyes locked in a smoldering gaze that was so intense, it took Claire's breath away.

"Aren't you going to kiss me?" she asked when she

could bear the look on his face no more. She spoke in a voice that wasn't her own. She wasn't even aware that she had been the one to break the silence.

Miles leaned over her. In the firelight, she could see his eyes flicker. "I'm going to kiss you in places you've never dreamed of being kissed," he told her sensually just before their lips touched.

Claire didn't have time to be afraid. As Miles caught her mouth with his own, she felt her body ignite. His passion was too difficult to resist, and she didn't even try. Instead, she let the tiny flames of desire licking her body grow larger and larger until she was shocked to hear herself moan.

The sound seemed to inflame him. He swept her off her feet, only to deposit her on the sofa in front of the fireplace.

"You're driving me wild," he muttered as he stretched out beside her.

Claire gasped as she felt the length of his body press against hers. Instinctively she turned so that she faced him. Her arms went around his neck and she wriggled closer to him.

Miles said something under his breath as she pressed against him. His hands were firm, yet gentle, as he turned her so that she was on her back.

"Not yet," he whispered unsteadily. "I want to touch you and I want you to touch me . . . everywhere." The word seemed to linger in the air.

She turned her head and opened her eyes long enough to see the naked longing in his face. Wonderingly, she stroked his cheek with her hand. His hot, wild eyes blazed back at her. They seemed to glint with flames that had nothing to do with the reflected light of the fireplace.

Suddenly, she smiled to herself. Why fight something that seemed so right?

Miles quickly deepened the kiss, and it wasn't long before their tongues were joined in an erotic dance. When their mouths finally separated, Claire was breathless and Miles was all but panting.

As if they had a mind of their own, Claire's hands snaked their way beneath his knit shirt. Her fingers glided through the coarse hair on his chest until they came to rest over his heart. It beat with such thundering strength and rapidity that it seemed to shake his rib cage.

"That's right," Miles muttered as his lips slid down her neck, leaving a little trace of goose bumps behind them. "Touch me. Get to know my body."

Claire responded by lightly running her hands over his chest. So intent was she that she barely noticed when Miles pulled her sweater off and sent it sailing through the air. Her blouse and bra quickly followed.

She felt a shock as Miles sat up to remove his own shirt and the cool air of the room touched her overheated skin. But before she had time to react, Miles was lying beside her again, and his hot, bare skin more than made up for the warmth that had been provided by her clothing.

For a moment, her hands wandered over his powerful shoulders. She could feel his muscles straining as he tried to control himself, as he tried to keep from rushing her or hurting her. Then he pulled her hands away from him and pushed her back so that he had full access to her body.

"Now it's my turn," he murmured provocatively. "You know what you do to me. Let's see what I can do to you."

Claire's eyes widened and showed alarm.

"Don't be frightened," he whispered as he read her sudden apprehension. "I want you to like this, Claire."

His words set off a warning bell deep in the recesses of her mind, but Claire was too caught up in the pleasure of the moment to pay much attention to it, and Miles was too expert a lover to give her much time to think.

"I'm not frightened," she murmured, and oddly enough, she wasn't. She closed her eyes and began to tremble as his hands moved slowly up her rib cage. When they covered her breasts, she gasped and her eyes flew open. Miles was watching her with a combination of passion and tenderness in his face.

He gave her a crooked smile, then bent his head and took one of her nipples in his mouth. When his lips touched the tip of her breast, hundreds of tiny explosions went off throughout her body. A sound that was part moan, part whimper came from the back of her throat. Miles heard it and immediately shifted his attention to her other breast.

"You're beautiful," he murmured. He propped himself up on his elbow and stared unblinkingly at the bare upper half of her body.

"I feel beautiful," Claire confessed with a little gasp. Her heart was beating so quickly, she was surprised she could even talk.

"You should," he told her huskily. "You're perfection in every way."

His eyes continued to devour her, and when he looked back at her face, he found she was blushing.

"You're not embarrassed, are you?" he asked gently.

"A little," she admitted. "No man has ever looked at me like this before."

"Good," he muttered gruffly. Again his free hand

started moving from one breast to another. He seemed fascinated by the effect he was having on her. "This is one part of you I have no intention of sharing."

He kissed her again and, with ease born of experience, sent her into a dark fog of sensuality. Claire stayed where she was, not thinking, only feeling, until she heard the unsnapping of her jeans. Even with the rain pounding on the roof above them and the wind howling around the house, the sound penetrated the sensual mist surrounding her and forced her back to reality.

"What are you doing?" she asked. Her body tensed as Miles slid his hand beneath her waistband and his fingers brushed her stomach. There was panic in her voice. A few moments ago, she had thought she was ready for this, but now she wasn't so sure. She had never made love with a man before, and she was a little frightened. Once she gave in to him, there could be no turning back. She had to be sure she was doing the right thing.

"Don't stop me," he muttered. "I want you too much to stop now." He began tugging at her jeans, trying to pull them down over her hips.

"No, Miles," she said in a voice that was practically a sob. "I can't."

He refused to let go of her. "It's too late," he told her determinedly. "Just relax and let it happen. Let me show you how wonderful it will be when our bodies—"

"No!" she said loudly and a little frantically. Somehow, she managed to get free long enough to slide off the sofa. Before he had a chance to react, she was halfway across the room.

"Claire!" he said. His voice rang out authoritatively above the storm outside. "Where are you going?"

She didn't turn to face him until she had picked up her

126

clothes and clutched them to her chest. They were her only protection against his eyes.

"To bed," she answered shakily. Something in his face made her add one word. "Alone," she said in a firmer tone.

Miles stood up. Claire tensed, but he didn't move toward her.

"Why?" he demanded angrily. "I thought—"

Claire winced. "I thought so, too," she said dully. Tears filled her eyes, and she felt more miserable than she ever had before. How could she explain all her fears to him? There were too many lies between them.

He stared at her, and as he took in her tousled hair and her wide, apprehension-filled eyes, his face softened.

"Claire," he began in a gentler voice. He held out his hand and moved toward her.

She didn't wait to hear what he had to say. She turned and bolted into the bedroom. When she reached it, she slammed the door behind her and leaned against it, breathing quickly. Her heart was pounding so loudly, she didn't hear Miles swearing in the other room.

Finally, she slipped into a nightgown and crawled miserably into bed. She pulled a couple of extra blankets over her, sure it would be hours before she fell asleep. She tossed and turned on the bed, her body tense, while she tried not to relive what had happened in the living room.

It wasn't long before she realized how chilly the little room was becoming. It was shut off from the warmth put out by the fireplace, and the cold wind of the storm whistled through every crack it could find. Even the warmth of the wool blankets wasn't enough to keep her warm.

This is ridiculous, she thought crossly. What was she doing in here by herself?

She sat up, wrapped her arms around herself, and stared into the darkness.

Face it, she told herself, you'd be a lot happier in the other room with Miles.

She rested her forehead on her knee. In spite of his lies, she was starting to fall in love with the man. She didn't want to fight him off any longer.

Then what was she doing in here by herself? she asked herself again. She dredged up all the courage she possessed and went into the other room. Miles was lying on the floor in front of the fireplace. She couldn't tell whether he was asleep or awake. She knelt down and touched him tentatively on the shoulder.

"Miles," she murmured before she could lose her nerve, "let me come into your bed."

He sat up. "Are you sure this is what you want?" he asked. His eyes were intent on her face.

"I'm sure," she whispered.

He reached up and gathered her to him.

Claire shivered a little as his arms enfolded her, but it wasn't from fear or nervousness. This was where she wanted to be, this was where she belonged. She raised her face to his, and as their lips touched, she felt a rush of happiness that only increased when he began to caress her. As their passion grew, so did her joy. When they were finally still, worn out from mutual transports of delight, Claire knew coming to Miles's bed had been the right thing to do.

She fell asleep believing they would have a future—together.

When morning came, the sky was bright and clear and the air smelled clean and fresh. Claire awoke to find herself still clasped in Miles's arms. She turned her head and looked over at him, her heart in her eyes. Asleep, the lines of his face seemed to disappear, and he looked young and vulnerable. As she stared at him, a sudden wave of tenderness washed over her. She leaned over and gently kissed him on the ear.

Miles's eyes opened, and he gave her a lazy smile.

"Good morning," he said. He reached up and pulled her head toward his for a long, slow kiss that Claire didn't feel like ending.

"Did you sleep well?" she asked shyly a few moments later. She didn't know what else to say.

"Very well," he answered. "In fact, I can't remember when I've slept as well. You're a good bed partner," he added with a grin. His smile grew larger as his words brought crimson to her face.

He let go of her and stretched. As the muscles on his chest rippled and contracted, he reminded Claire of a panther. He was as dangerous as a panther, too, she told herself. Making love hadn't changed the lies he'd told her. A little nervously, she slid from beneath the blankets.

"How about you?" he wanted to know. "How did you sleep?"

"Very well," she answered brightly. She smiled down at him, hoping he wouldn't see how flustered she suddenly felt.

"If you have any aches or pains from sleeping on the floor," he told her mischievously, "I'll be happy to massage them away." He held out his arms. "Come on back down here. I've been told my hands can work miracles."

For a moment, she was tempted. Oh, how she was tempted! But they had to get back to Charleston. "That's not necessary," she told him. "I don't have a single ache or pain anywhere." She moved purposefully toward the kitchen.

"Too bad," he commented regretfully. "I would have enjoyed getting rid of them for you. Maybe we can invent an ache or two."

She laughed. Now that she was out of the reach of his arms, she felt more confident. "I think we'd better be getting back to town. I'll make some coffee while you take a shower."

He sighed. "You're a hard woman," he told her as he headed toward the bathroom.

What will happen next? Claire asked herself as she measured the coffee into an old percolator that had seen better days. She might be naïve, but she wasn't naïve enough to think that Miles would now own up to all his lies. Last night, making love had seemed so right; now it just seemed to have complicated things. Miles was still lying to her, and she was still trying to find out his plans. But now she had to deal with her feelings for him as well.

An hour later, after a hasty breakfast of coffee and toast, they were back on their way to town.

"Your beach house was a big success," Miles told her as they drove back across the marshes. "I had a wonderful time. We'll have to go back soon."

"I enjoyed it, too," Claire said shyly.

He reached over and covered her hand with his. "You look a lot more relaxed this morning," he said. "Getting away from that house of yours obviously does you good. You should do it more often."

"As a matter of fact," she told him, "I *am* going to be getting away for a while."

He glanced at her in surprise. "Oh?" he asked. "Where are you going?"

"Hawaii," she answered.

A grin spread on his face. "Hawaii," he repeated thoughtfully. "Don't tell me you're going to the National Association of Small Hoteliers Convention?"

She looked at him in surprise and nodded.

"What a coincidence," he said with obvious satisfaction. "So am I."

Claire's heart leaped within her. Seeing Hawaii with Miles would be wonderful. Then something tightened in the pit of her stomach. Seeing Hawaii with Miles would be . . . dangerous. There was no other word for it. Last night she had faced the fact that she was falling in love with him. Now she had to face the fact that the more time she spent with him, the greater her hurt would be if their relationship came to an end. And that seemed very likely, she thought with a sudden pain in the region of her heart. How could she plan on anything permanent with a man who couldn't be truthful with her?

"But why are you going to this convention?" she wanted to know. "I'd think you'd send someone on your staff." A sudden thought assailed her. "You're not going because I am, are you?"

He shook his head. "No, although I can't think of a better reason. I'm going because I've been asked to give a talk on the economies of small hotels—how to cut down expenses and increase profits. I've been branching out lately, and I own four successful small hotels."

"Oh," Claire said. She looked away. That was one of the seminars she had especially wanted to attend.

"I'm leaving on Wednesday afternoon," Miles was saying. "You can fly over with me on my corporate jet."

"I don't think so," Claire said quickly. She suddenly

felt she had to put some distance between them. "I've already made airplane reservations, and—"

"Cancel them," Miles interrupted. He obviously didn't intend to take no for an answer.

She shook her head doubtfully. Spending all those hours alone with Miles, she was thinking, could either be a wonderful experience or an excursion to disaster. She didn't think she wanted to risk it. He had too much power over her as it was.

He took his eyes off the road and glanced over at her. "Think of all the time and money you'll save by going with me," he said. "Especially the money. Plane fare to Hawaii is pretty expensive, you know."

"I know it is," she said helplessly. "It's just that . . ." she stopped, feeling utterly miserable.

Miles took one of his hands from the steering wheel and placed it over hers. "Haven't I proven to you that I can be trusted?" he asked quietly. "Didn't last night tell you anything?"

Claire took a deep breath. "It isn't you I don't trust," she confessed suddenly. "Last night, I—" She broke off, aware of the color that had flooded her face. "You confuse me," she finished lamely.

He squeezed her hand. "At least that's a step in the right direction," he said lightly. Then his voice grew serious. "I don't want to force you into my bed," he told her. "I want to wait until you feel the same way about me as I feel about you."

She didn't answer. How did he really feel about her? He hadn't mentioned the word *love* since that night in her garden. Now that she wanted to hear it, he seemed to have conveniently forgotten all those things he had said to her. Had he meant anything he said that night?

All at once, she realized what she was thinking. Horrified, she shrank away from him and stared out the window. There could only be one reason why she wanted to hear his declaration of love, and that was because she had done what she had sworn she would not do.

She had fallen in love with him. She had fallen in love with the man she was supposed to be spying on, the man who had come to Charleston to wreck her life and her happiness. She was so shaken by that thought that she missed most of what he was saying.

"—and we'll fly from Charleston to Atlanta where we'll board my jet," he finished up confidently. As far as he was concerned, she hadn't objected to his plan at all.

"That's fine," she murmured faintly.

Miles glanced at her quizzically. Confidence aside, he hadn't expected her to agree so quickly. Then he mentally shrugged. He had learned long ago not to quarrel with a good thing.

When they reached her house, Claire leaped out of the car and headed for the kitchen. She wanted to get away from Miles and back into the comfortable routine of her day-to-day life. Maybe that way she could forget all this nonsense about being in love.

Sarah was in the kitchen, just starting the dishes. Her face brightened when she saw Claire.

"I fed your hungry guests," she began cheerfully. "It wasn't the best breakfast in the world, but at least they didn't starve." She abandoned the dishes and perched on the edge of the table. "I've been on pins and needles waiting for you to get home. What did you find out?"

"Find out?" Claire echoed. She looked blankly at her friend.

"About Miles and his plans," Sarah said with a trace

of impatience. "That's why you took him out to the beach—to find out his plans. Remember?"

Claire nodded reluctantly. She remembered all too well. "I didn't find out much of anything," she said, not wanting to admit that she and Miles hadn't discussed his plans at all.

"Why not?" Sarah asked.

Claire shrugged her shoulders and began loading the dishwasher. "He's very vague," she said, "and he doesn't seem to trust me. He says he hasn't made up his mind about what he wants to do. He claims he's thinking of refurbishing an old hotel or opening a small inn. That's all I know."

"That's not what Michael says. Do you think he's telling the truth?" Sarah asked.

Claire shrugged. "Who knows? I'm sorry I don't have anything else to tell you, but I warned you before, I'm no Mata Hari. This isn't going to work."

"Of course it will," Sarah told her briskly. "You've just got to try a little harder. All men like to talk about themselves. I'm sure Miles is no exception."

Claire shook her head wearily. She wished she'd never agreed to Sarah's crazy scheme, never started this deception in the first place. She didn't want to spy on Miles any longer.

"I'm sure he hasn't given up his idea of a hotel in Charleston," Sarah was saying, "or he would have left town. You'll just have to spend some more time with him. Somehow you'll have to get him to talk."

"He's going to the NASH convention," Claire said reluctantly.

"That meeting you're attending in Hawaii?" Sarah asked.

Claire nodded. "He wants me to fly over with him on his corporate jet."

"That's wonderful!" Sarah exclaimed delightedly. "You'll be alone together in the small cabin of his jet for hours! Anything can happen."

That was exactly what Claire was afraid of.

"We'll run him out of town yet," Sarah said with satisfaction. She looked down at her watch. "I've got to run. I have an appointment in a few minutes. I'll talk to you later."

"Thanks for this morning," Claire called after her. She stared at the half-filled dishwasher without seeing it. A terrible thought had just struck her.

If they did succeed in running Miles out of town, as Sarah put it, she'd probably never see him again. But if she didn't try and stop him, he would be in a position to hurt the town she loved so much. In either case, it seemed she was going to be the loser.

CHAPTER EIGHT

Their plane swept in over a jade green lagoon, then touched down at Honolulu's bustling airport. As they came in for a landing, Claire stared at the lush green land in fascination. Hawaii was every bit the paradise everyone said it was.

Outside the airport, a cream-colored Mercedes sports car, with its top already down, was waiting for them.

"You do travel in style," Claire said as she slid into the car.

"It's the only way to travel," he said with a grin.

"It's not the only way," she retorted, thinking of the budget flight she would have taken and the crowded bus filled with travel-weary tourists that would have transported her to her hotel. "But I'll admit it's the best." She sat back and let the wind ruffle her hair as they drove to the hotel where the convention was being held.

At the hotel, she left Miles in the lobby and followed the bellhop up to her room. It was, she thought a little ruefully when she saw it, probably the smallest and least expensive room the hotel had to offer. It barely held a bed and dresser. However, she hadn't wanted to spend money she needed for her house on anything more expensive.

Besides the minimal furniture, the room was filled with

sweetly scented, tropical flowers. Claire picked up the card in front of one of the bouquets and glanced at it. Then she picked up another card and another. By the time she had read each card, she was smiling. All the flowers were from Miles.

She reached for the phone, intending to call and thank him. Then her eyes fell on the luggage the bellhop had left just inside her door. Somehow, Miles's briefcase had gotten mixed up with her things and had ended up in her room.

On impulse, Claire put down the phone, picked up the briefcase, and made her way to Miles's room.

He'd be worried about losing it, she rationalized as she hurried down the hall to the elevator. Besides, she had to thank him for all those beautiful flowers. She didn't want to admit to herself how much she wanted to see him again—even though they couldn't have been apart for more than a half hour.

At his door, she hesitated for a moment, then knocked resolutely. She was suddenly a little nervous. He opened the door and she held up his briefcase.

"This was delivered to my room by mistake," she said crisply.

He gave her a warm smile and took it from her. "Come on in," he invited.

Claire tore her eyes from his and forced herself to look past him. What she saw made her gasp with delight.

"This is beautiful!" she exclaimed as her eyes traveled around the spacious living room furnished with comfortable furniture upholstered in tropical colors. Her eyes stopped at the huge expanse of windows that led to a balcony overlooking Waikiki Beach. It was a spectacular view by anyone's standards.

Miles took her by the arm and gently pulled her inside. "If you like that view," he said wickedly, "you'll love the one from my bedroom."

Claire began to laugh. She couldn't help it. Miles's suite made her room look like a closet. "You should see my room," she said as she caught his questioning look.

"I'd like to," he said promptly. Claire ignored the insinuation and the sudden gleam in his eye.

"Oh no, you wouldn't," she told him. "Compared to this, it looks like a hole in the wall."

"Does it have a bed?" he asked meaningfully. "That's all I care about."

"It has a single bed," she told him mischievously. "There isn't room for anything large."

"We could make do with a single bed," he said easily. "Lovemaking doesn't require a great deal of room, you know."

At his words, Claire felt her cheeks grow warm. The conversation was getting a little out of hand. She decided to steer it back to safer waters.

"At least you won't be crowded," she said neutrally. "I've never seen such a large suite."

He shrugged and moved toward the bar. "Is your room really that small?" he asked as he turned on the blender for a few seconds, then divided the delicious-looking liquid between two glasses.

"It's even smaller," Claire said cheerfully.

He frowned. "I'll call the desk and have them find you something else," he told her.

"No, don't," Claire said as he reached for the telephone. "I don't need anything larger, and I certainly wouldn't want to pay for it. Besides, I won't be doing anything but sleeping there."

"If I have my way, you won't even be doing that," Miles said lazily.

One look at his face told Claire he meant exactly what he said. However, she was suddenly feeling too light-hearted to be upset by his words or the meaning behind them. She was in Hawaii, and she was going to enjoy herself. So she merely smiled at him and held out her hand. "Is one of those for me?" she asked teasingly. "Or are you expecting someone else?"

He studied her face for a moment, then smiled back. "It's for you," he said as he handed her a glass of fruit juice. "I thought we'd take it out on the balcony."

"This is heaven," Claire said as she stretched out on a comfortably padded chaise. "I don't think I'll do anything but lie in the sun and sightsee while I'm here."

Miles raised his eyebrows. "What about the seminar and the meetings?" he asked a little mockingly. "I thought that was why you came."

"It was," she admitted as she watched the surfers. "But now that I'm here, I just want to relax and enjoy myself."

"Then we'll play hookey together," he told her. He wasn't looking at the surfers or the view; he was watching her instead.

"You can't do that," she objected, though she knew that was exactly what she wanted him to do. "You're one of the speakers. You have to attend the meetings."

"Only some of them," he said airily. "Believe me, I'll make sure I have plenty of time for you."

Claire turned toward him. When their eyes met, she felt her heart jump. "Good," she murmured a little shyly. "I'd like that."

Miles's eyes darkened perceptibly, and he lifted his

139

hand to gently caress her cheek. Claire gazed back at him, her eyes wide and vulnerable. For a moment, she thought he was going to kiss her, but he didn't. Disappointed, she relaxed against the back of her chair and took another sip of the delicious juice he had prepared.

"I'm having a small cocktail party early this evening," he said, "but it shouldn't last long. Why don't you plan on attending? When it's over, we'll go out to a romantic little place I know of for dinner."

"You *would* know of a romantic little place for dinner," Claire told him.

He merely smiled. "Then afterward," he told her, "we'll let nature take its course."

Claire was following her own thoughts and only half heard his words. "This is certainly the place for romance," she murmured dreamily. He looked over at her and his face changed.

"Claire," he said in a voice that sounded half strangled.

She looked over at him and color flooded her face. She quickly swung her feet to the floor and got up. "I've got to unpack," she said, "and I still haven't registered for the convention."

The strained look left his face. "All right," he said indulgently. "Run away for now. But don't forget about tonight."

Claire lifted her eyes to his. "I won't," she said simply. Before Miles could say another word, she left him.

That evening, she arrived at Miles's cocktail party just as it was starting to break up. He saw her the minute she walked in the door.

"I thought you had decided not to come," he told her a little angrily.

140

Claire glanced at him in surprise. "I fell asleep on the beach," she said. "I'm sorry I'm late. I didn't think you'd miss me."

His annoyance eased a little. "Well, I did," he told her. "In fact, I was just getting ready to come to your room to look for you." His face tightened. "I've never been stood up before, and I don't intend to start now."

Claire put a hand on his arm. "I wasn't going to stand you up," she said with compunction. Then her voice grew stronger. "Though it probably wouldn't hurt you if I did. It might teach you a little humility."

"Oh, do you think so?" he asked irritably.

She studied his face. He obviously wasn't in the mood to be teased. "No," she confessed with a sigh. "I don't suppose it would."

She was beginning to feel uncomfortable. This wasn't the lighthearted banter she had been daydreaming about. Miles seemed annoyed, upset, and completely unromantic. Suddenly, she felt dejected. To think I was actually looking forward to tonight, she thought unhappily.

"Do you think I could have something to drink?" she asked, trying not to sound as miserable as she felt. She didn't want him to see how his attitude depressed her.

"You can have one at the restaurant," he said abruptly. He took her arm and steered her toward the door.

"But what about all these people?" she stammered as she looked around her. "You can't just walk out on them."

"I can and I'm going to," he said as he held open the door for her. "They can see themselves out."

"But—" she began helplessly.

"Don't argue," he snapped.

It was the last thing either of them said until they were

in the car and driving through the balmy evening air. Then Miles gave her a smile and a look that would have melted a glacier.

"I'm sorry," he said ruefully. "I know I was a little hard on you back at the hotel, but I wanted to have you all to myself."

At his words, Claire felt her heart stop. Then it rebounded suddenly, making her a little giddy.

"You were a little irritable," she said in her most neutral voice.

"I was sick and tired of making polite small talk with people I'd never seen before when all I wanted was to be alone with you," he confessed.

Claire turned her head and gazed at his profile. The lines around his eyes and mouth had disappeared, and he looked completely relaxed.

"Well, here we are," she said lamely.

"And from now on we'll concentrate on us," he finished the thought.

Her smile deepened. Why not? she thought to herself. Why not?

All through dinner, she felt the two of them were living under some kind of romantic spell. They laughed and talked and held hands like teen-agers.

After dinner, when they returned to their hotel, the spell could have broken, but it didn't.

"Come up to my suite," Miles urged her as they took a last-minute stroll around the hotel garden. They stopped in the shadow of a tall old tree and he pulled her close. "Spend the night with me. I promise you won't regret it."

Claire was tempted. Each time he touched her, she was more tempted. But she knew she needed time away from him. She was afraid the passion that erupted between them might consume her if she didn't have a break from him now and then.

"Not tonight," she said softly. "It's been a long day, and I'm tired."

Miles stared down at her through the darkness, and his mouth drew close to hers. "All right. But let me show you what you'll be missing. I want you to think about this while you're alone in your bed."

His lips hungrily claimed hers. He kissed her with a force that left Claire breathless. As he gently forced her mouth open and began to explore it, Claire felt her body respond in ways she had never imagined. She leaned against him, glorying in his strength and power.

"Miles," she whispered when his lips finally relinquished hers and began moving down her neck. The ache in her voice reflected the aching of her body.

"Are you sure you want to go up to that small single bed of yours?" he asked hoarsely. "Think of what we could be doing in my bed with nothing between us, not even the sheets."

At his words, Claire couldn't help moaning softly. In her mind's eye, she *could* see the two of them in his big bed. She could almost feel his hands, unencumbered by clothes, on her body. The very thought made her dizzy.

He seemed to follow her imaginings with uncanny precision.

"I want to lay you down on my bed," he told her thickly, "and peel off your clothes one by one. I want to kiss every inch of your gorgeous body. Then, when all your clothes are off—"

With a little cry, Claire broke away. She couldn't stand much more of this. His words were about as stimulating as the movement of his hands. She stood just out of reach, staring at him in the darkness. His breath was coming as unevenly as hers, and she could feel her heart pounding relentlessly against her rib cage. Hoping to slow it a little, she put a hand over her breast. Miles followed the movement with hungry eyes.

"How much longer are you going to keep this up?" he demanded angrily.

"I don't know what you're talking about," Claire protested unsteadily, though of course she did know. She couldn't blame him for being angry. She wasn't being fair to him any more than she was being fair to herself. If only she could forget all the lies that stood between them, she thought miserably. If only she could let her heart rule her head.

Miles must have seen the unhappiness and indecision in her face.

"All right," he said more gently. There was obvious resignation in his voice. "I'll walk you to your room and leave you at the door." A light flashed dangerously in his eyes. "After all, we still have two more nights before we have to go back to Charleston."

Claire had just gotten out of the shower when the phone rang. With only a towel wrapped around her, she ran out to answer it, hoping it was Miles. It was.

"Since you wouldn't spend the night with me," he said as soon as she answered, "at least you can come up for breakfast. It will be ready in fifteen minutes." He hung up before she could say anything.

She glanced at the clock, gathered the towel more tightly around her dripping form, and went back into the bathroom to finish drying off. Fifteen minutes later, she was knocking on the door to Miles's suite.

He opened it, looking as immaculate as ever in white slacks that showed off the powerful lines of his legs and a pale blue shirt that emphasized his broad shoulders. As soon as she saw him, she was immediately aware of the fact that there hadn't been time to completely dry her thick hair and that her sundress was distressingly ordinary.

Miles, however, didn't seem to find anything amiss.

"Good morning, beautiful," he said as his eyes slid down her body. He leaned over and planted a lingering kiss on her mouth. "You look good enough to eat."

"I'm afraid you'll have to settle for breakfast instead," she said in a slightly brittle voice. She walked around him, and as he closed the door behind her, she saw that breakfast was already set up on the balcony.

"I was waiting for you before I got started," he said as they sat down at the table.

"I'm overwhelmed!" she told him as she looked at the array of delicious-looking fruits the waiter had brought up. There was also an assortment of hot, fresh pastries, several pitchers of juice, and coffee and tea. "I've never seen so much food for two people."

"I didn't know what you'd want, so I had them bring up a little of everything."

"And it's all been prepared by someone else," she said blissfully, thinking of the pineapple she hadn't wrestled with and the juice she hadn't squeezed. "What a wonderful way to begin the day."

"I think breakfasts at your house are a pretty wonderful way to start the day," he said as he passed her a bowl of fruit.

"That's because you don't have to get up early and fix them," she said.

145

"You wouldn't have to either," he told her, "if you'd—"

"Let's not talk about that," Claire said hastily. She didn't want to discuss selling him her house. Not now. Not when everything was going so perfectly.

"All right," he said equably. Then his voice dropped slightly. "I know of an even more wonderful way to begin the day," he informed her.

"What's that?" she asked. She looked across the table at him, and something in his face made her cheeks flush wildly.

"Waking up in the same bed," he informed her wickedly. "What could be more wonderful than that?"

Nothing, Claire thought before she had a chance to consider what was racing through her mind. Fortunately, she didn't say it out loud. Miles didn't need that kind of encouragement.

"All last night I dreamed you were with me," he went on in an even lower voice.

Claire tore her eyes from his and stared down at the flakey croissant on her plate. She'd tossed and turned with the same kind of dreams, but she wasn't going to admit it.

"When I woke up this morning," he added regretfully, "I was holding a pillow in my arms. It made a poor substitute."

Claire ate a small piece of mango without tasting it. It was high time to talk about something else.

Miles, however, wasn't finished. "It was a soft pillow," he went on, recapturing her eyes and holding them by sheer force of will, "but it didn't have any curves, and it didn't have the feel of your silky skin. Are you going to

146

make me sleep with only a pillow for company again tonight?" he demanded urgently.

Claire tried to break through the tension that seemed to be holding her spellbound, but she couldn't. It was as if the urgent intensity of his eyes were hypnotizing her, forcing her to speak the truth.

"I don't know," she whispered after a moment. "I don't know."

Something she couldn't read flickered across his face. "I want you to belong to me, Claire," he said. He watched her with a strange expression on his face. "I've wanted it since the first moment I saw you, and now I'm running out of patience. I've waited a long time for you to realize that we belong together. Don't make me wait much longer."

That sounded like a threat to Claire. She didn't answer.

"Would you like to hear the plans I've made for us today?" he asked after a moment.

"How could you make plans?" she asked. She poured some coffee into a cup and wrapped her hands around it. Even in the sunshine its warmth felt comforting. "According to the schedule, you're speaking at one of the seminars this afternoon."

He shook his head. "I *was* speaking at one of the seminars this afternoon," he corrected her matter-of-factly. "But I called Mike Johnson, the person in charge of the program, and told him I was only free this morning. The whole afternoon is ours."

"I don't understand," Claire began, but he cut off whatever objection she was going to make. "Then tomorrow, I thought we'd fly over to Maui for the day."

"Maui?" she asked.

He nodded. "It's a beautiful island, and there's a pine-apple plantation-turned-hotel there that I want you to see. Unfortunately, we'll have to be back in time for the banquet," he added regretfully. "I couldn't get out of that."

"Why not?" Claire asked dryly. "You don't seem to have had trouble getting out of anything else."

"As a matter of fact, I'm getting an award for the hotel I'm going to show you on Maui," he told her. There was a twinkle in his eyes as he watched to see the effect his words would have.

"The National Association of Small Hoteliers is giving Hotels Americana an award?" she asked incredulously. "I don't believe it."

"They're not giving it to my corporation," he pointed out. "They're giving it to me. Not everyone thinks my hotels are as bad as you seem to think they are."

Claire ignored that. "I think I'll lie on the beach this morning," she said. "That's something I never get to do at home."

"I wish I could join you," he said regretfully. "Lying on the beach with you sounds like a lot more fun than what I'm going to be doing. However—"

"Duty calls," Claire finished for him.

"That's not what I was going to say. I was going to say that after this morning you won't be out of my sight."

He smiled at her, and after a moment she smiled back. She couldn't help it. Miles could be irresistible when he wanted to be.

"Don't fight it," he told her softly. "It won't do you any good."

Her smile deepened, and she shook her head. "You're incorrigible," she told him as she got to her feet.

"That's why I succeed where others fail," he said. "That's why I'm succeeding with you. Aren't I?"

Claire looked at him with laughter in her eyes. "Maybe," she said noncommittally.

He got to his feet and started to move toward her. "Claire," he began somewhat unsteadily.

She took one look at his face, gulped, and quickly made her way to the door. "I'll be ready at noon," she threw over her shoulder. As she closed the door, she could hear Miles muttering behind her. She was glad she couldn't hear what he was saying.

Instead of going back to her room, a sudden impulse took her down to the boutique in the hotel lobby. If she was going to be sitting at the head table tomorrow night, she owed it to herself to look great. The dress she had brought to wear to the banquet was nice enough, but it was very ordinary, and it definitely belonged at a table in the back of the room. Besides, she told herself, trying to rationalize the money she was about to spend, she'd saved a lot on air fare by flying over with Miles. She could easily afford a new dress if she wanted one.

Forty-five minutes later, she walked out of the boutique in a daze. A kind of madness had come over her when she looked at all those beautiful clothes. That was the only explanation for it. Why else would she have bought three dresses when she had only meant to buy one? And at those prices, too!

In her room, she opened the box that held the dresses and shook out the sarong that she had chosen to wear to the banquet. As she hung it in her closet, all her doubts vanished. Even though it was nothing more than an exorbitantly priced piece of colorful silk that knotted over her breasts, it did amazing things for the way she looked.

For the first time, she admitted to herself that Miles was the real reason for her purchases. She wanted him to find her beautiful, irresistibly beautiful.

He did.

"You look ravishing," he told her when they met in the lobby at noon. His eyes took in her new backless sundress and the way her strappy sandals emphasized her lovely legs. "In fact, you look much too wonderful to sit in a hot car. Let's go back to my suite and have our picnic in air-conditioned comfort."

Claire laughed. She was delighted at the look in his eye, delighted at the way the expression on his face made her feel.

"Oh no," she said lightly. "You promised me a tour of the island, and that's what we're going to do."

"I'd much rather tour your body," he murmured in a voice designed to turn her bones to water.

Claire blushed and looked around to see if anyone had heard. She hadn't expected him to be so outspoken.

"First things first," she said, giving him a saucy smile.

She heard his sudden intake of air and looked up to find him regarding her quizzically.

"Woman," he said after a moment, "you're driving me crazy. I suppose you know that."

He cupped her chin with his hand and raised her head so that he could look into her eyes. Claire gazed back at him, feeling a little giddy. By teasing Miles, she was playing with fire, and she knew it. Suddenly, though, it didn't matter. She loved him, and they were together. That was all that counted.

His eyes darkened as he looked at her. "I see," he said. "You *do* know it."

She laughed and pulled away. "Shall we go?" she asked.

Miles jammed his hands into his pockets and stared at her. At the expression on his face, her heart began to pound erratically, and she was glad they were standing in the lobby. If they had been alone, she knew she would have found herself in his arms and that resistance would have done her no good whatsoever.

"Be careful," he warned her in a thickened voice. "I can only take so much teasing. After that . . ."

Over the pounding of her heart, she managed another laugh. She turned and started toward the doors that led outside. A second or two later, she felt Miles's hand on her bare back. His touch jolted her, and for a moment she was as sorry as he was that they were going sightseeing.

The next day and a half passed almost magically. They laughed and talked, and though Miles occasionally watched her broodingly, he did nothing more than kiss her a few times. He seemed to be biding his time, though for what Claire could not imagine.

They flew to Maui, where he showed her his small hotel. Claire could see at once why it was being given an award. Impressed though she was, however, she couldn't see that kind of setup in Charleston.

By a kind of tacit consent, they avoided discussing business. Claire didn't want to be reminded of what had brought him to Charleston, and he didn't seem to want to remind her. Neither did she want to remember that she was supposed to be worming her way into his confidence and discovering his plans. The very thought of the deceitful role she had undertaken chilled her.

She dressed with care for the banquet, though aside from slipping on some panties and tying the sarong, there really wasn't much dressing to do. When she was finished, she eyed herself in the mirror with satisfaction. Even to her own eyes, she looked wonderful—and completely unlike the conservative Claire Ashley that Charleston knew so well.

She brushed her hair till it shone, then plucked an orchid from one of the bouquets Miles had sent her and pinned it over her ear. The flower brought out the sparkle in her eyes and made her face glow.

"I've never seen you look more lovely," Miles told her when she had shyly opened the door to her room. "I bought you these," he said, nonchalantly tossing some more flowers on the bed, "but you don't need them. You're perfect the way you are."

"You're looking very handsome yourself," she told him to cover the shyness she was suddenly feeling. Besides, it was true. In his well-fitting evening clothes, he looked very masculine and totally desirable. He seemed to fill her small room, to overwhelm it—and her—by his very presence.

"I'd like to take you in my arms and kiss you," he told her. "But if I do, I won't be able to control myself, and we'd never make it to the banquet." His eyes flickered dangerously. "For two cents, I'd give up the banquet and the award—"

"And you'd regret it later," Claire told him.

"Would I?" he asked. "I doubt it. Some things are more important than a plaque with my name on it, and you're one of them."

"Well, I'd regret it," Claire said firmly. She preceded him through the door, aware of the way her silken sarong moved and clung to her as she walked. Miles was aware of it, too, she knew. She could feel his eyes on her as they made their way to the elevator.

All during the banquet and the award ceremony, Miles sent her dark, brooding looks that first nonplussed her, then made her nervous. As soon as it was possible for them to leave, he hurried her out of the banquet room, through the lobby, and into the elevator.

"There's a bottle of champagne waiting for us in my suite," he said as he pulled her along with him. "This is our last night in Hawaii. We're going to make the most of it."

As they rode up in the elevator, he draped an arm over her bare shoulders. Through the fabric of his coat she could feel the erratic pulse of his heart. Her own pulse began to beat erratically in response.

When they were alone in his suite, Miles seemed to relax a little. He pulled his tie off and shed his coat, then expertly opened the champagne bottle with just the right amount of pop. Next he lowered the lights, led her over to the large overstuffed sofa, and handed her a tall, graceful glass filled with champagne.

"To us," he said as he eased his long body down beside her. In the dim light, he clinked his glass against hers.

"I thought we were here to celebrate your award," Claire said breathlessly. She knew the award was the last thing on his mind at the moment. It was just about the last thing on her mind as well.

"I'd rather drink to us."

Claire took a sip of champagne, hoping it would moisten her suddenly-dry mouth. They sat in silence for a moment or two longer; then Miles suddenly put his glass on the table in front of them and deftly removed hers from her hand.

"We don't want to spill it, do we?" he asked. There was a rich undercurrent of laughter to his voice.

"No," she stammered.

He leaned forward and gathered her into his arms. Claire went without a protest.

"No more stalling," he said just before their lips joined. "We've both waited long enough for this night."

He kissed her with devastating forcefulness. Claire felt her body incline toward him, then suddenly they were stretched out on the soft, deep sofa.

"You're a fast worker," she gasped as soon as she had the chance.

"I have to be," he answered thickly. "I don't intend to let you get away this time."

He slid a hand under her head and turned her so that their lips met again. This time her mouth opened, and he nibbled at the sensitive inner skin of her lips. Claire felt the room fade away, and she raised her arms to encircle his neck and pull him closer.

Miles muttered something under his breath, but she didn't have the faintest idea what it was. She brushed her fingers across his face and watched his eyes open in response. The expression in them was one of obvious desire combined with tenderness so sweet that it nearly brought tears to her own eyes.

Miles didn't give her much time to think about what she saw in his face. Instead, he began trailing a fiery line of kisses down her neck and across her bare shoulders. As he moved closer and closer to the curve of her breasts, Claire began to tremble. One part of her wanted to stop him, but the other, more insistent part was clamoring for him to go on.

With a sure move, Miles removed her arms from around his neck and propped himself up on one elbow.

"I want to touch you," Claire heard him mutter. Her eyes were closed. She was afraid of what she'd see in his face if she opened them.

She felt his free hand move to the knot over her breasts that held her dress together. Her heart went wild as he lazily untied it. When the knot was undone, he slowly pushed the fabric aside and gazed down at her. All she was wearing beneath the dress was a pair of lace panties.

"Perfection," he breathed after a swift intake of air. His hand gently traced the line of her body.

At the sound in his voice, Claire opened her eyes. He was staring down at her body with an expression so intense that she could scarcely bear it.

He touched her breast possessively, then bent to take a nipple in his mouth. As his lips touched her sensitive skin, she felt something twist inside her, and a tiny moan forced its way up from her throat.

"Don't fight it," she thought she heard Miles say. "Just relax and let it happen."

"I can't relax," she managed to say. "Your hands are doing strange things to me."

"And this is only the beginning," he told her. His own breath was coming as unevenly as hers, and she could hear the strain he was under in his voice.

He slid his hand down the length of her body to the lace banding of her panties. His fingers sensuously slid under the lace and began easing the wisp of fabric over her hips. Claire gasped as his hand moved lower and lower.

"You're so beautiful you make me ache," he told her.

"I know how you feel," she answered in a shaky voice. "I ache too."

"Do you?" he whispered ardently. "Let me take care of that ache for you."

He swept her into his arms, carried her into the bedroom, and gently put her on the bed. As he pulled his clothes off, he stared down at her with an unblinking gaze that sent shivers through her. Then he dropped down next to her. With impatient hands, he reached for her and began kissing her wildly. He couldn't seem to stop.

Claire kissed him back, welcoming his hands as they moved up and down her body. Finally, when she was lost in a sensual mist, when she was no longer aware of what he was doing, he entered her. Claire felt herself being lifted to the stars.

When they finally came back down to earth, Miles gently brushed the hair away from her face. He gave her a triumphant look. "Admit it," he whispered. "You put up quite a struggle, but I won in the end. I finally got what I wanted from you."

Without another word, he rolled over and fell asleep. Claire was left staring into the darkness in shock. All her worst fears were suddenly being realized.

Then her shock changed to anger. He was nothing more than a callous, insensitive brute, she thought as her anger grew. So he thought he'd won! We'll see about that! she told herself grimly.

She slipped out of bed, tied her sarong around her, and headed for the door. Miles didn't seem to notice she had gone.

CHAPTER NINE

Claire and Miles traveled home in almost complete silence. Miles sat hunched over some papers at a small table in the front of the airplane's cabin while Claire curled up in a chair and stared at a book, pretending to read. In the wee hours of the morning she had come to a decision, and now she was planning how to tell him about it.

It wasn't until about an hour before they would land that Miles put away his work, leaned back in his chair, and stretched like a large, lazy cat.

"I didn't mean to ignore you," he said with a smile that made Claire's heart turn over. "But I've really been letting the work pile up."

"I understand," Claire said stiffly. She wished her heart hadn't been so quick to rebound like that. She took a deep breath to steady herself. "You know," she said more slowly, "there's something I want to discuss with you." This wasn't going to be easy, she thought to herself, but it had to be done.

"What is it?" Miles asked. He got to his feet and went over to the small galley for a club soda. "Would you like some?"

Claire took it gratefully. It seemed like a long time

since the steward had served them lunch. Besides, it gave her something to hold on to, something to focus on, and she had a feeling she was going to need it.

"Now, what do you want to discuss?" Miles asked. He sat down in the chair beside her, and her anxiety increased. Why did he always make her feel like this? she asked herself angrily.

"I'm going to have to ask you to move out of my house."

Miles looked at her with raised eyebrows, making her even more nervous than before.

"It's not because of what happened last night," she rushed on nervously. "It's just that I need your room starting tomorrow night for some people who reserved it several months ago." She stopped and took a sip of soda water.

"I see," he said calmly enough. She got the idea he had been expecting something like this. His eyes were intent on her face, but she had no idea what he was thinking. His own face was completely unreadable. "And after they leave?"

"It's booked by someone else, and someone else after that," she said, looking him straight in the face. She'd always read that a lie should be told as convincingly as possible, and she was giving it her best try. "I'm sorry," she added, "but summer is my busiest time, and I had no idea you'd want the room indefinitely when I accepted their reservations. You do understand, don't you?"

"I understand."

"Good," she said with uneasy relief. "I don't want you to think I'm asking you to leave because—"

"Because we've been lovers," he finished silkily.

Claire stared down at the bubbles in her club soda. She

knew she'd be glad for something to focus on! "Well, yes," she told him, hoping she sounded convincing.

That, of course, was exactly why she had asked him to leave. Feeling the way she did, she couldn't bear to have him under her roof any longer. Last night had shown her how vulnerable she was. She couldn't, *wouldn't,* run the risk of any more heartache than she had already let herself in for.

"I'll just move into a hotel," Miles told her quietly.

"You mean you're not leaving Charleston?" she asked cautiously. She'd half expected him to tell her he was leaving town now that he'd gotten what he wanted.

He looked at her in surprise. "Of course not," he said. "I still have some work to do, and we still have things to discuss."

Claire's heart stood still. Was he finally going to ask her to sell her house?

"Have you found any property in Charleston that interests you?" she asked diffidently. She had decided to try to find out all she could during their flight home. He may have gotten what he wanted from her, but she hadn't gotten what she wanted from him.

"As a matter of fact, I have," he said, leaning back and crossing his ankles. "I received some very interesting reports while we were in Hawaii." He gave her a thoughtful look, then he grinned mischievously. "Not everyone is the die-hard preservationist you are."

"Do you mind if I ask what those leads are?" she asked even more diffidently still.

"No, I don't mind," he said lightly. His grin deepened. "But I don't think I'll tell you. I'll let you be surprised like everyone else."

159

Claire looked at him suspiciously. What could he be planning now?

"Are you glad I'm not leaving Charleston?" he asked.

It was a transparent attempt at changing the subject, Claire thought. She shrugged. "I'd like us to be friends," she said quickly.

He burst out laughing. "Friends and lovers," he told her with a chuckle. "But never just friends."

The Fourth of July dawned hot and humid. Claire, who had been invited to a half dozen picnics, barbecues, and parties, spent the day instead working on one of her third-floor bedrooms. Miles had moved into a hotel with a minimum of fuss, just as he had said he would. He was the reason she had turned down the invitations to the Independence Day celebrations being held all over town. She was sure he'd been invited to the same parties, and she didn't want to see him. Somehow, she had to put him out of her heart and her mind, and there was no time like the present to start.

In fact, ever since his move some four or five days ago, Claire had been avoiding him. Either that, or he had been avoiding her. She wasn't quite sure which.

All she knew was that he hadn't called or come by and that she missed him terribly. Once or twice she had been tempted to call him, but pride had stopped her. If he couldn't be bothered to call her, she certainly wasn't going to call him!

How has my life managed to get so complicated? she asked herself as she furiously scraped off layers of dull, faded wallpaper. Only a few months ago, things had been so simple. All she'd had to worry about was finding the money for her house. That had never been easy, but at

160

least it wasn't fraught with peril. Now she had a host of things to worry about, not the least of which was her relationship with Miles.

Then there was Sarah, she thought as she vigorously attacked a fresh patch of wall. When she'd returned from Hawaii, she'd been relieved to learn that Sarah was in Savannah on business. That meant Claire didn't have to report her failure to find out Miles's plans, and it also meant she didn't have to face Sarah's sharp eyes. Sarah would take one look at her and know she was in love with Miles, and that was something she didn't want to talk about—not to Sarah, not to anyone.

Dusk was beginning to fall when she heard someone knocking on her front door. Who could that be? she wondered a little irritably. She had given all her guests keys so they could come and go at will. She sighed. One of them must have lost his, she thought as she stiffly made her way down the stairs.

When she opened the door, however, she didn't find one of her guests standing on the loggia. Instead, she found Miles gazing down at her and looking very pleased with himself.

"Hello," she said repressively, trying not to sound as delighted as she felt.

"Good evening," he answered in his smooth urbane voice. "Aren't you going to invite me in?"

Claire reluctantly opened the door so that he could step inside.

"As you can see, I'm fairly busy," she began crisply.

His eyes took in her plaster-flecked hair and her wallpaper-sprinkled skin in one sweeping glance. Claire was wearing very short cutoffs and a T-shirt, and she felt very exposed and very grubby.

161

"What are you doing?" he asked, "tearing down the house bit by bit?"

"Hardly," she answered. "I'm stripping off wallpaper in one of the bedrooms."

There was a twinkle in his eyes. "I hoped to see you at the festivities today, but when you didn't come, I thought you might be avoiding me," he probed.

"Of course not," Claire said indignantly. "Why would I do that?" His observation flustered her because it was true.

He shrugged. "I can think of several reasons you might want to avoid me," he told her.

She gave him an even look. It was time to turn the tables. "As a matter of fact," she said loftily, "I had the feeling you were avoiding me."

He didn't bother to deny or confirm that. "We're together now," he said instead. "That's what counts. Now come into the garden and see what I've been doing."

Claire followed him through the house a little suspiciously. She hadn't even realized he'd been in the garden! When they reached the door leading outside, her eyes went past him and widened in surprise. The iron table that graced her small terrace had been set for two, complete with a long flowing cloth, china, crystal, and a tall, elegant silver candelabrum. There were even fresh flowers to scent the air.

"What *is* all this?" Claire asked as she stepped outside. Now that the sun was going down, the temperature seemed a lot milder. It was going to be a beautiful, balmy evening.

"Dinner," he replied succinctly. "I wanted to have dinner with you, and this seemed to be the best way for us to be alone."

162

Alone.

The word seemed to reverberate around the garden. To be alone with Miles was the one thing Claire didn't want. She especially didn't want to be alone with him in such a romantic setting.

"But . . ." she stammered. For a moment, she was at a loss for words. Then she got hold of herself. "You're assuming a lot, aren't you?" she asked coolly. "How do you know I don't have other plans for the evening?"

He didn't seem the least bit put out by her sudden coolness. "For one thing," he drawled, "I doubt you'd be going out like that." His eyes flicked over her.

That really made Claire angry. "Just because I'm not dressed yet doesn't mean I don't have a date with someone else," she snapped.

Miles looked at her quizzically through the gathering dusk. "Well, do you?" he asked.

Claire looked up at him, and her anger suddenly dissolved. It was hard for her to stay angry with him when he looked at her like that. "No," she admitted with a sheepish grin, "I don't.".

"Good," he said simply, "I'm glad."

All at once, she was glad, too, and it showed in her face. Miles touched her cheek gently and gave her a warm smile.

"Why don't you go change into something a little more romantic?" he suggested. "That sarong you had on the other night will be perfect."

Claire was glad the gathering darkness hid the sudden pink that stained her cheeks. She wasn't about to put on something that would remind her of his insensitive remarks that night in Hawaii. Without replying, she turned away.

"While you're gone," he said, "I'll go in the kitchen and get the food ready."

Claire turned back. "You won't find anything to eat," she said ruefully. "I was just going to have tuna salad for dinner. I doubt there's anything else to eat except the things I need for tomorrow's breakfast."

"Don't worry," Miles said, gesturing toward a picnic basket near the door. Claire hadn't seen it on the way out. "I brought our dinner with me. I knew if we had to depend on your pantry that we'd end up in a restaurant surrounded by people, and I didn't want that."

Claire didn't want that, either. Now that he was here, she realized how starved she had been for the sight of him. She didn't want to share him with waiters and other diners. She wanted him all to herself.

"You're very good at anticipating," she told him breathlessly.

His eyes met hers for a long, lingering moment, so intense that Claire felt as if she had just been kissed. She swallowed hard. "I always try to be one step ahead," he said meaningfully.

Again Claire turned to go. She couldn't bear to look into his eyes any longer.

"Hurry," Miles ordered from behind her. "I don't like waiting."

Forty-five minutes later Claire had showered, washed, and dried her hair and changed into an old-fashioned white cotton lawn dress that would have been at home at a turn-of-the-century afternoon garden party.

"You look stunning!" Miles exclaimed as she stepped shyly into the garden.

He held out his hand, and Claire, after only a moment's hesitation, put her own hand in it. As if she were a

164

rare and priceless article, he led her over to the table and seated her. The candles had been lit, shedding a mellow glow, and the stars were beginning to shine above. Claire thought her garden had never looked so romantic, and she had never felt so romantic.

"Everything looks wonderful," she murmured dreamily as Miles lifted a bottle from the silver ice bucket standing near the table. "Champagne?"

"The king of wines," he answered. Slowly he poured it into her glass. "I didn't think we deserved anything less."

"How did you manage all this?" she asked once he started serving the chilled lobster salad, the fresh French bread, and the ripe melon slices. "You must have gone to a lot of trouble."

"You're worth it," he told her.

He leaned over and brushed her cheek with his lips. Claire felt a little shiver work its way down her spine.

"I wanted this to be a special evening for us," he added. "After we eat, we can walk down to the Battery and watch the fireworks."

"We don't need to do that," Claire said. It was an impulse she hoped she wouldn't regret. "We can see them from the roof of the house."

He lifted his eyes and gazed at her. "Without other people around us," he said softly. "That's a wonderful idea." He poured her another glass of champagne, then pushed the bottle firmly back into its bed of ice. "We'll save the rest for later. It'll go well with the fireworks."

Claire stared back at him with tremulous eyes. Her mouth was suddenly dry and her stomach full of butterflies. What had she gotten herself into? she wondered with a surge of panic. Then she noticed the warmth of Miles's face, and the tenderness of his smile, and she wondered no longer. For better or for worse, she was in love with him, and that was all that mattered.

By the time they had finished eating, it was completely dark. Miles scooped up the wine cooler and their glasses and followed her through the house and up the stairs to the roof.

"This is perfect," Miles said with satisfaction as he looked around him. "But we need a blanket."

Claire looked startled. "A blanket?" she began doubtfully. "But—"

"You can't sit down here," he told her smoothly. "You'll ruin your dress. And I'm sure you want to watch the fireworks in comfort. It won't be as much fun if we have to stand." He moved toward the stairs that led down to the attic. "I'll find one. You just enjoy the evening."

While he was gone, Claire stared at the winking lights of Charleston. It was a fairy-tale panorama. For the first time, she realized just how alone she and Miles were up there. No one would walk in on them, and no phones would ring. They might as well be the only two people in the world. Claire shivered a little.

Then Miles was back. In his arms he was carrying a blanket, which he put down first, and a soft, fluffy quilt, which he spread on top of the blanket. Then he lowered himself onto the quilt and gently pulled Claire down with him. She sat beside him, very conscious of his warmth and vitality, and nervously smoothed her dress over her knees.

"Champagne?" he asked. Without waiting for an answer, he splashed some into her glass and handed it to her.

Claire took it and put it down beside her, untasted. She

didn't want to drink it. She was already feeling giddy, though she knew that feeling had nothing to do with the wine.

"When do they start?" he asked.

"Any minute now," she answered breathlessly.

"Good," he said. He stretched out his legs and leaned back on the quilt. "Though I don't suppose we'll really need them," he added lazily as he reached for Claire.

"What do you mean?" she asked. She was suddenly lying down, her head resting on his arm.

"I mean we're going to make our own fireworks tonight," he answered quietly and implacably. He looked over at her. "I see skyrockets explode every time I kiss you. I doubt if anything manmade can compare to that." With lazy strokes, he began caressing her hair.

"I know what you mean," Claire whispered after a moment. The words seemed to come out of their own accord. "I see the same thing you do."

Miles's eyes glinted suddenly and dangerously in the moonlight. "I was beginning to wonder if you'd ever get around to admitting that," he told her roughly.

"There they go!" Claire said as a burst of silver sparkles suddenly danced across the sky. "Look, Miles."

Miles didn't bother to turn his head. "I don't need to. I can see them reflected in your eyes," he murmured. He started tracing the lines of her face with his finger. It was almost as if he wanted to memorize the feel of it.

Claire was beginning to have trouble with her breathing. Miles's eyes, intent and probing, refused to leave her face. She tried to ignore him and concentrate on the brilliant colors lighting up the sky, but it was impossible. She turned and let his eyes capture hers.

"You're missing something spectacular," she told him. Her hand went to his face, and she touched it gently.

"Not any more, I'm not," he muttered. "Not after to-night."

Her breath caught in her throat as he leaned toward her. Then his lips were on hers, and the world began to slip away. When his tongue pushed its way into her mouth, she forgot about the fireworks overhead and the fact that they were lying on a blanket on her roof. Nothing seemed to matter but Miles and the way he made her feel.

Claire let him draw her close, and this time when he kissed her, she kissed him back feverently. Her mouth opened, and he began exploring it, making her tremble.

"That's right. Don't hold anything back," he encouraged her as her arms went around him and she held him. "If you do, you'll be cheating both of us."

"Miles," she managed to murmur. She could barely hear herself over the pounding of her heart.

He silenced her with his lips. "This is our night for passion," he whispered against her mouth. "I've been wanting to make love again since our last night in Hawaii."

His hands moved up her rib cage to her breasts. Through her thin cotton dress Claire could feel the heat of his palms. She gasped as he began to stroke and stimulate the sensitive skin. A moment later, she turned in his arms and pressed herself against him with abandon.

"I like the way your body feels next to mine," she confided shyly. The boldness of her words surprised her. She peeked through her lashes at him just long enough to see the effect her words had on him. His eyes glinted

168

dangerously in the light of the spangled sky, and his mouth twisted with suppressed hunger.

His arms tightened around her until they were lying thigh to thigh, breast to breast. Slowly, almost lazily, his hands moved down to her hips. Then he deliberately pulled her hips against his, making Claire gasp at the intimate contact.

"It gets better," he told her in a voice as smooth as honey. Gently his lips touched her face, creating shivers of sensation.

"It can't get better," she managed to say. She was beginning to have trouble with her breathing, so much trouble that she doubted if she'd ever talk again.

"Oh, but it does," he murmured hoarsely. "I promise you that." With fingers none too steady, he began unbuttoning her dress. After a few frustrating moments, the number and size of the buttons seemed to enrage him. He swore out loud, causing Claire to open her eyes and stare at him in wonder.

"What is it?" she whispered. His face was flushed, and little beads of sweat were forming across his forehead.

"You wore this dress on purpose," he rasped hoarsely. "You knew these tiny buttons would drive me mad."

Claire brushed a trembling hand across his face and laughed. Her laughter tinkled softly and seductively through the night as he eased the dress up over her head. His eyes widened, and he sucked in a lungful of air as he looked down at her. He reached for her, but Claire lifted her hand and held him back.

Miles's eyes narrowed. He obviously thought she was going to stop him. "Don't you remember how it was in Hawaii?" he asked. "Don't you remember how you felt when I untied your sarong and took your breasts in my mouth?"

Claire blushed and her heart went wild. "I remember," she murmured. An ache was welling up somewhere deep inside her.

"Don't you want to feel it again?" he demanded seductively. "I do. I'm not going to let you stop me."

"I'm not going to stop you," she said in a voice so low he had to strain to hear it. "I just want you to take off your shirt so I can touch you, too." She loved Miles, and no matter what happened tomorrow, she was going to have at least one night of memories.

Miles's eyes flashed. "You little seductress," he murmured.

A second later, his shirt went sailing through the air, and Claire was running her hands across the thick dark hair that covered his chest. As her hands slid down through the curls that led to his waist, she felt his body shudder with pleasure.

"Do you feel what you do to me?" he asked urgently.

Claire nodded, her eyes wide with wonder.

"Now I'm going to do the same thing to you," he said hoarsely. "I'm going to make you tremble and burn with desire."

"You already do," she told him with a seductive smile. "You do things to me you can't begin to imagine."

"Claire," he muttered in a tortured voice, "my Claire." He didn't seem to be able to say anything more.

Deftly he unhooked her lacy bra. It joined her crumpled dress, and a moment later, so did her panties.

"Don't think about anything," he cautioned her as if

170

he were still afraid she would pull away. "Just let your-self feel the magic between us."

Claire had no intention of pulling away. Instinct was taking over, and she began to strain toward him. Her hands went to his belt buckle, but she found she couldn't undo it. Miles pushed her hands away and unbuckled it himself. Claire didn't know how he managed; she only knew a shock of pleasure when his bare legs tangled with hers and his hips pressed her back against the blanket.

Her hands slipped restlessly down his back until they came to the muscular smoothness of his buttocks. Claire pressed them close, and the closeness made her shift longingly beneath him.

"Don't," he cautioned her in a voice she had never heard before. It sent shivers through her.

She could tell he was close to losing control. It gave her a feeling of power that she had never felt before, and again she shifted her body teasingly beneath his. As she did so, a low moan tore out of his throat. The sound both shocked and excited her.

"If you do that one more time," he rasped. "I'll take you right now. I can't wait much longer."

Claire opened her eyes and was immediately sorry she had teased him. The strain of holding back was apparent in his face.

"Why wait?" she whispered as her heart beat a tattoo against his chest.

"I want this to last as long as possible," he whispered against her mouth. He couldn't seem to stop kissing her —not even to talk. "I want you to remember this for-ever."

His hands slid down her body and between her thighs.

171

Claire jumped at the contact, and he opened his eyes long enough to see the response of her body to his touch.

"Let yourself go. Feel me touch you. Enjoy it," he coaxed.

She didn't answer. She could barely breathe, let alone reply.

His lips slid up her body to her mouth. The kiss he gave her was long and slow and sweet. Claire's heart was beating so frantically, she thought she might die.

"Miles," she moaned, not even aware that she had spoken. A burst of wild excitement went off inside her.

"I want this to be perfect," he muttered as he pressed her soft body against his own hard contours.

"And I only want to please you," she whispered back. A nameless longing was sweeping over her, and she didn't know how much longer she could contain herself.

"You do," he breathed in a voice as taut as his body. "You do."

Gently and slowly, he lifted her to him. Instinctively, she arched toward him.

"That's right," he encouraged her in a voice that was almost at the breaking point.

Claire barely heard him. When he entered her, her entire body was consumed by a burst of pleasure that was pure and intense.

"Claire . . . Claire," Miles murmured over and over as his body reached its glorious climax and began to relax against hers. "You're wonderful. And this was as wonderful as I knew it would be."

"Perfection," she said softly.

They stayed where they were, letting a long, fulfilled silence stretch out between them. Claire stared up into the sky, where brightly colored stars and spangles filled the sky, but she was so absorbed by what had just happened to her that she didn't even notice. A strange lassitude was overtaking her. All she wanted to do was stay like this, with Miles's body next to hers, forever.

Finally, he shifted his weight slightly.

"I'm not too heavy for you, am I?" he asked. His gaze swept across her flushed face.

She smiled up at him, a lazy seductive smile. "Why don't you kiss me again?" she murmured invitingly. "Then I won't notice."

He leaned over and kissed her with reverence that she hadn't expected. Her eyes filled with tears, and she suddenly felt warm and cherished. She lifted her hand and gently stroked his face. Her eyes, as she stared up at him, were shining.

Miles chuckled suddenly, and his laughter sounded rich and triumphant. "I will kiss you again," he promised, "and again, and again. In fact, I plan on kissing you all night long."

"That sounds heavenly," Claire told him a little shyly. Her sense of modesty seemed to have disappeared.

"It sounds like my idea of heaven, too," he admitted. "But first I think I'd better get you inside. The next time we make love, we're going to do it properly, in a real bed. I don't want you to get any bruises on that delicious backside of yours."

In spite of everything, Claire couldn't help blushing at his words.

He stood up and tenderly lifted her, quilt and all, into his arms.

"What about our clothes?" she asked as he made his way down the stairs to the third floor of her house.

173

"We'll get them tomorrow," he told her. "Right now I have something else in mind."

He carried her into her bedroom and kicked the door shut behind them.

CHAPTER TEN

"Good morning," Claire said shyly when Miles finally woke up the next morning. She had slipped out of his very firm hold on her a few minutes earlier and was already dressed.

"It'd be a better morning if you'd come back to bed," he mumbled. Sleepily, he reached for her.

Claire laughed and avoided his outstretched arms. "I've got to get breakfast ready for my guests," she said. "I forgot all about them last night."

Miles sat up and gave her an appreciative look. "You had more important things on your mind," he told her. "Any regrets?"

"No," she whispered. "No regrets."

At her words, Miles bounded out of bed. Claire's breath caught in her throat as she took in the long, lean lines of his very masculine—and very naked—body. He grinned wickedly as he saw her eyes widen; then he took her gently in his arms.

"I'll only let you go if you promise to come back as soon as you've finished breakfast," he told her as his hands made a slow langorous movement down her back.

"I've got the dishes to do and—" she began.

"Leave them," he commanded. "The dishes can wait—

I can't." His voice became more persuasive. "Besides, I want to show you how exciting love in the morning can be."

"You mean you want to . . ." Claire's voice faltered, then trailed off. She was suddenly a little embarrassed.

Miles laughed. "Yes," he said wickedly. "I want to. Again and again and again." He bent over and kissed her. It was a gentle kiss, but there was an insistence behind it that Claire could not miss. "Do you mind?"

Her breath caught in her throat. "No," she whispered softly. "I don't mind." She found herself wishing her guests could fix their own breakfasts. Her hands went to his chest and tugged their way through the thick coils of hair.

He caught her hands and held them away from his body. "Don't do that," he warned her, "or I won't be able to let you go."

Claire gave him a tremulous smile and stepped away. "I'll be back before you have time to miss me," she told him.

"I doubt that," he replied. His eyes were ardent. The look in them made Claire glow from head to foot. "I miss you already. After last night, it doesn't seem right not having you in my arms."

"I'll be back as soon as I can," she promised again. She backed toward the door, trying not to be dazzled by his masculinity.

"I'll be waiting," he replied. He seemed totally unconcerned by the fact that he was standing in her bedroom with absolutely nothing on.

Claire flew down the hall and into the kitchen. All the things she usually did the night before, such as setting the table, were still undone. She hummed as she worked, feeling so happy that she doubted her feet were even touching the floor.

Things are going to work out for us, she told herself determinedly as she squeezed some fresh juice. She loved Miles, and she wasn't going to let any of the nagging doubts that were lurking at the back of her mind destroy her happiness.

After breakfast was over, she had just dumped the dishes into the sink and was preparing a tray to take up to Miles when the back door opened and Sarah stepped inside.

"Hi," Sarah said. "I haven't seen you since you got back from Hawaii, so I thought I'd stop in and—" She broke off suddenly and stared at Claire. "What's going on?" she asked curiously. "I've never seen you look so radiant."

"Nothing's going on," Claire said at once. "How was Savannah?"

"Savannah was Savannah," her friend replied impatiently. "More important, how was Hawaii?"

"Very nice," Claire answered lamely. "The convention was interesting. There were some very good speakers who—"

"That's not what I mean, and you know it," Sarah broke in. "I want to know about Miles Sinclair. What were you able to find out about his plans?"

Claire shook her head. "Nothing," she said quietly. "He didn't tell me anything." Thank goodness Miles had promised to stay upstairs. If he heard Sarah . . .

"Honestly, Claire!" Sarah was saying with more than a little exasperation in her voice. "How hard can it be to get a little information out of the man? I would have wormed it out of him weeks ago."

177

"That's probably true," Claire conceded stiffly, "but I'm not you. And I'm certainly not any good as a spy."

"You're just not trying hard enough," Sarah told her, suddenly changing tactics. "I know you don't like the man, but this is for a good cause."

"I have tried," Claire said tiredly. How had she gotten mixed up in this? "And it won't work. He has no intention of confiding in me. He told me so himself."

Sarah waved away Claire's words with a simple gesture. "Wine him and dine him," she advised. "If that doesn't work, try a little flattery, a little romance. He won't be able to resist that."

Again Claire shook her head. She wished she had never agreed to go along with Sarah's little scheme.

"You don't want him to put up one of his detestable hotels here, do you?" Sarah asked.

"No, but—" Claire began.

Sarah overrode her. "Then you've got to get busy. I've heard rumors that he's found other property to buy. But no one seems to know where it is or whom it belongs to. If *you* don't find out—and soon—we won't be able to stop him."

Claire sat down at the kitchen table. She was going to have to tell Sarah that she couldn't spy on Miles any longer, that no matter what he told her, she couldn't betray him.

"Invite him over for a candlelight dinner," Sarah went on. "Afterward, take him into the living room, dim the lights, and pour him some good cognac." She sent Claire a penetrating look. "You might even let him kiss you a few times," she added. "After that, he's sure to talk."

Claire pushed her chair back from the table and stood up abruptly. She had to tell Sarah she had no intention of pumping Miles for information, and she had to tell her now.

She was just about to speak when she heard a sound in the dining room. A terrible thought hit her. She pushed open the door from the kitchen just in time to see Miles leaving the room. With sick certainty, she knew he had overheard enough of their conversation to think the very worst. Her heart plummeted, and all her dreams for the future crumbled like ashes.

Beside her, Sarah gasped and her mouth fell open. Claire paid no attention. She felt as if the very life was draining out of her.

"Miles," she called. "Wait. Let me explain."

He turned to face her, and she held out an imploring hand. He ignored it.

"I've heard enough," he said bitterly.

"No," she cried. "You don't understand." She could see her dreams dying in front of her. She took a step toward him, but the look on his face stopped her. As she stared at him in mute anguish, she could feel her heart break.

"I understand," he told her coldly. "I understand all too well."

He gave them both a withering look, turned on his heel, and stamped out of the room. Claire watched him go without moving a muscle. She might have been turned to stone.

He left a shocked silence behind him. Claire couldn't move; she couldn't even speak.

It was Sarah who broke the silence. "I had no idea," she said faintly. She sat down in one of the dining-room chairs and gestured toward the door. "Is that why you looked so radiant this morning?"

179

Claire didn't answer. Large tears began sliding down her cheeks.

"You're in love with him," Sarah said slowly. There was a note of discovery in her voice. "Aren't you?"

Finally Claire nodded.

"Then go after him," Sarah urged her. "Explain. Make him understand!"

The front door slammed, and Claire winced. Miles hadn't wasted any time getting dressed and out of her house. And out of her life. She groped blindly for a chair and sat down in it.

"I can't," she said dully. "How can I possibly explain?"

"You can," Sarah said firmly, "and you've got to. If you really love him, you can't just let him walk out of your life." Her voice grew gentler. "I'm sorry, Claire. I had no idea."

Claire brushed the tears from her eyes.

"How does he feel about you?" Sarah asked.

"I don't know," Claire told her wearily. "How should he feel after this?"

"Does he know you love him?" Sarah pursued.

"No," Claire admitted after a moment.

Sarah stared at her friend thoughtfully. "Go," she said finally. "Find him and talk to him. You'll never forgive yourself if you don't at least try."

"You're right," Claire said suddenly. Even though she felt as if something had just died inside her, she knew she had to explain to Miles. She wouldn't be able to live with herself if she didn't.

Without another word, she left Sarah sitting in the kitchen and hurriedly walked the few blocks to Miles's hotel. At the hotel, she didn't wait to be announced. Instead, she went straight up to his suite.

When she knocked on his door, a snarled "come in" from inside the room told her that Miles was even more angry about what he had heard than she had realized. She swallowed hard, which wasn't easy considering the lump in her throat, and pulled the door open.

"Did you come to try and use your feminine wiles on me again?" he asked in a hard, bitter voice. His eyes were dark, narrow slits filled with contempt. "If you did, you're wasting your time."

"I don't blame you for being angry," she managed to say, "but—"

"Angry?" he laughed mirthlessly. "That one little word doesn't begin to describe how I feel."

Claire stepped inside the room and pulled the door closed behind her. It took all her courage to perform that simple act. Miles looked so furious that she was tempted to turn and run.

"How do you feel?" she asked as steadily as she could.

"Like a fool," he snapped. "Like every kind of a fool." He turned away from her abruptly and resumed his packing.

Even though Claire knew she had been dismissed, she held her ground. She stared silently at his back for a moment, wishing she knew what to say, wishing she knew how to begin. Furiously, she blinked back the tears that were filling her eyes. Crying wouldn't help.

"That's how felt when I found out why you had come to Charleston," she said finally.

"That was different," Miles said at once. The words were tossed over his shoulder in clipped tones. He didn't even bother to turn and look at her. "I didn't come here

181

to take advantage of you. But you," his voice grew contemptuous, "you knew how I felt, and you deliberately used those feelings to try and find out my plans."

"That's not true," Claire cried. Anger suddenly spirited through her. Why was she having to justify herself? After all, Miles was the one who had created this situation in the first place.

He swung around and stared at her. His eyes were cold and implacable. "I don't think there's anything more to say." He looked past her pointedly. "You know the way out."

All at once, Claire saw beneath his anger, and her own anger evaporated instantly. The things he had overheard had hurt him far more deeply than she realized.

"Before I go," she said gently, "I want to explain. I want to make you understand—"

"Well, I don't want to listen," he interrupted roughly.

"You may not want to, but you're going to," Claire said doggedly. "Because I'm not leaving until you've heard what I have to say. Unless, of course," she added in an attempt to lighten the atmosphere, "you decide to throw me out."

Something she couldn't interpret came and went in his eyes. "Don't tempt me," he said briefly.

Claire looked over at him and sighed. He was standing with his arms crossed, staring down at her with a face that might have been carved from granite.

"When I found out why you had come to Charleston—" she began quietly.

"Why had I come to Charleston?" he interrupted.

"To buy property for a hotel," she answered. "I found out that you wanted to buy my house in particular."

182

"Just to set the record straight, I gave up that idea the first day we met," he told her.

"Why didn't you tell me?" she wanted to know.

He shrugged. "Once I'd decided not to build a hotel, I didn't see any point in talking about it."

She stared at him, then returned to what she'd been saying before he interrupted her. "When I found out why you said all those things to me that night in the garden, I was hurt, very hurt. You said you had fallen in love with me. Then I found out you hadn't been telling the truth. You had been lying to me."

"I didn't lie to you," he said.

"You did," Claire said tiredly. "You lied about why you were in Charleston, then you lied about the hotel you were thinking of building. You lied about practically everything. That was when I decided to try and find out what your plans were," she went on miserably. "I thought it wouldn't hurt you to get a little taste of your own medicine."

Miles's face grew even harder. Claire stole a look at it, and her misery increased. She knew, she just knew, that he would never forgive her. Nevertheless, she forced herself to go on.

"Don't you see?" she asked a little desperately. "I was hurt in a way I had promised myself I'd never allow myself to be hurt. I was hurt because a part of me wanted to believe what you had to say. A part of me wanted to trust you. Then once I found out you had lied, I was afraid to trust you."

He unfolded his arms, jammed his hands into the pockets of his pants, and walked restlessly over to the window.

"And that's when you decided to get even," he said as

183

he stared at the people walking on the sidewalk below. It wasn't a question. It was a statement. He sounded as if he already knew the answer.

Claire winced. "I suppose that's one way of looking at it," she said reluctantly. "But I didn't think of it as 'getting even.' I thought of it as a way of protecting something I love. And then . . ." Her voice faltered and came to a stop.

He turned and looked at her intently. "And then what?" he prompted.

Claire took a deep breath and looked straight at his collarbone. She couldn't bear to look him in the eyes. What she saw there hurt too much.

"And then I realized that I couldn't spy on you, I couldn't trick you into telling me your plans, no matter how much Charleston meant to me."

"Why not?" he asked in a voice that was quiet and still. His eyes were unblinking as he waited for her answer.

"Because I fell in love with you," she answered tiredly, "and once that happened I knew I could never betray you."

Miles didn't answer, and Claire felt another wave of tears fill her eyes.

"I don't blame you for being angry and I don't blame you for thinking the worst," she said, feeling emotionally drained. "But I couldn't let you leave town without trying to explain."

Still he didn't say anything, and Claire turned away without looking him in the face.

"I'll go now," she said. She stumbled toward the door, blinded by the tears she refused to let fall.

Miles reached the door before she did and blocked her

way. "Where do you think you're going?" he demanded in a voice that was no longer cold and distant.

Claire felt her heart slam against her ribs. "Home," she whispered in an uncertain voice.

"Not yet," Miles told her firmly. "Not until we get everything out in the open."

He swung her up into his arms and carried her over to the sofa. Still holding her tightly, he sat down. Claire stayed where she was, not moving, barely even breathing. Hope was beginning to blossom within her.

"Even now you don't believe it, do you?" he asked. There was a new warmth in his voice.

"Believe what?" she wanted to know.

"That I love you," he answered impatiently. "You still don't believe that I fell in love with you the first minute I saw you."

"Your business," she began. She looked up at him through lowered lashes.

"To hell with my business," he said succinctly. "It isn't nearly as important to me as you are." There was sudden frustration in his voice. "Why is it so hard for you to realize that?"

Claire shook her head. "I don't know," she whispered. "I want to believe you."

"Then do. Everything I said to you that night is true. You've *got* to believe me."

"I'm trying," Claire murmured. Her eyes were beginning to shine. "Maybe it would help if you told me again."

His grip on her tightened, and he pulled her close. "I love you," he whispered in her ear. "I've loved you since the first moment I saw you."

She rested her head against his shoulder and began to

185

relax against him. She had never been so full of happiness.

"I know love at first sight isn't rational, but where you're concerned," he went on, "I'm not a particularly rational man. I love you and I want you in my life always."

A dark thought floated across her mind and was immediately reflected in her face. "Are you sure making love isn't all you want?" she asked uncertainly. "I mean—"

He cut her off with a swift kiss that did a great deal to dispel her doubts. "Of course I want to make love to you," he answered a shade impatiently, "but I want more than that. I want you in bed with me every night, and I want to wake up next to you every morning. I love you, Claire."

"I love you, too," she murmured in return. She snuggled up to him, reveling in the feel of his strong arms around her. "I think I must have started falling in love with you the first day we met. I was just afraid to admit it to myself. When I heard you wanted to buy my house and turn it into a hotel . . ." She shuddered.

His arms tightened around her convulsively. "We seem to have been working at cross purposes," he said somberly. "You were afraid to trust me, and after what I heard this morning, I was afraid to believe in you. When we're married—"

"Married?" Claire repeated. She sat bolt upright and stared at him with wide eyes.

"Married," he repeated firmly. "Don't sound so surprised. Of course we're going to be married. Now that I've found you, I'm certainly not going to risk losing you."

186

"But you haven't even asked me," Claire murmured. Her soft blue eyes were luminous.

Miles reached up and gently touched her face. "That's easily remedied. Will you marry me, Claire?" he asked softly. "I love you, I want you, and I need you."

For the third time since she had entered Miles's hotel suite, tears filled her eyes. This time, though, they were tears of happiness.

"Yes," she whispered, "I'll marry you. I'll marry you and move to Chicago with you if that's what you want."

His eyes darkened, and she could see that he was touched by her offer to leave the home she loved so much.

"The ultimate sacrifice," he murmured teasingly. He began kissing her hungrily, as if he couldn't get enough of her. "That won't be necessary," he told her in between kisses. "I can run my business from here."

"You'd do that for me?" Claire asked wonderingly. She pulled away slightly and gazed up at him.

"That and more," he answered simply. "I want to make you happy."

"You have," she whispered. "You have."

Time began to dissolve for Claire as Miles worked his magic on her. She cuddled against him, glorying in the kisses that made her feel equally desired and cherished.

"Miles," she said breathlessly a few moments later, "what about your hotel?"

"My hotel?" he echoed. He opened his dark eyes and gave her a blank stare. His mind was obviously not on business. He leaned forward and caught her lips with his. "I've bought the old Ravenscroft place outside of town," he murmured against her mouth.

Claire knew immediately what he was talking about.

The Ravenscroft plantation had stood forlorn and empty for the past few years.

"It'll cost a fortune to restore," she exclaimed as Miles began trailing hot, swift kisses down her neck. She couldn't help shivering with delight as she spoke.

Miles lifted his head for a moment. "I don't want to talk about anything to do with hotels," he informed her. He began to slowly and provocatively unbutton her blouse. "In fact, I don't want to talk about anything at all."

His hands touched her bare skin, and Claire felt a wild rush of desire.

"Whatever you say," she managed to murmur before excitement claimed her.

Then a long, satisfying silence filled the room, and Claire knew she had found the one person who would truly make her house a home.